THE SEVENTH SISTER

A VAMPIRE ROMANTASY NOVEL

PARCHED
BOOK TWO

Z.L. ARKADIE

FLAMING
HEARTS

ISBN: 978-1-942857-58-7

 Formatted with Vellum

THE FOG

ONE

Riley Simms kicks the back of my chair for the third time in forty-five minutes. The first two times, I turned to glare at her, and she gave me a smug look. I'm way too bored to expend the energy necessary to bring her the satisfaction she seeks.

Mr. Cleotis Lux—yes, that's his real name—is going on about the Coriolis Effect. My eyes dart over to the wall clock. The long hand has barely inched forward. I hear it *tick... tick... tick...* at a turtle's speed. We may be in here forever.

"It's when matter that moves in a systematic, rotating pattern deflects off that set path," Mr. Lux says with his back to the class, marking a pattern in blue on the whiteboard.

Snow lies over the land beyond the windows that run along the wall to my left. Air flowing out of the vents makes it difficult for me to concentrate on Mr. Lux's boring lecture on the Coriolis Effect. My eyelids could drop at any second, sending me past daydream land into actual dreamland.

"Mr. Lux," Bill Lintner, the class suck-up, calls with his hand raised and fingers wiggling.

There's a low groan throughout the classroom. A few students throw looks at Linter, who defiantly straightens his posture and focuses even more on Mr. Lux's back.

"Doesn't the Coriolis Effect control the rotation of sunspots?" he asks without permission to speak. He's clearly showing off.

Mr. Lux's hand stops shading a line that's supposed to be the wind. He drops his arm to his side. My eyes focus on how the tip of the marker remains a few millimeters away from the seam of his black trousers.

He always wears black from head to toe. The color is striking against his blue eyes and deep tan skin. At times, he doesn't even look real, which makes him an object of fascination for every teenage girl—and those beyond their teen years—at

Bishop High School. Even me to a certain extent. My interest isn't romantic, but I wonder why he's the way he is.

For instance, from day one, he's never looked at me. That's not all in my head. My teacher has seriously never put his eyes on me—maybe once or twice, but that's all. He doesn't talk much to anyone, despite Bill Lintner's efforts to get him to elaborate on the assignments after every class.

Once I swear I heard him say, "*Do not do it*," inside my head. I had been trying not to listen to Riley Simms go on about how Derek Firth confirmed she's the hottest girl in the school.

"Hotter than *her*?" Riley's little sidekick Morgan Slater had asked.

"You're hotter than that toad." Riley laughed.

I had felt their eyes on my back. I wanted to shove my palm smack dead in the middle of her mouth. I actually considered the fallout. What would happen to me? I'd get expelled again? News flash: I don't care!

"So are you two going out now?" Morgan had asked. But Riley didn't answer right away.

"You know, I don't know what's wrong with the boys in this school. They all have bad taste. I mean, she's so ugly. Isn't she?" Riley asked, totally off subject.

"Who are you talking about?" Morgan asked.

"Who do you think? She's right there."

I knew she had shoved a finger toward my back. In that moment, I made a choice to do it, to put myself out of my misery, however mediocre it was. That's when I heard Mr. Lux's voice in my head, scolding me.

The man is just weird—but not in a gross way —in a fascinating way. Like right now, he's still just standing there with his back to us. Maybe this time he'll answer Bill's question. I have noticed that eventually he always gets to whatever Bill spouts off about at some later point in the lecture.

Everyone is extra quiet. The suspense is killing us. *Will he or won't he acknowledge Bill?* This is the most exciting moment since the bell rang and we opened our books to page thirty-two.

As we sit on the edge of our seats, I feel another shove against the back of my chair. This time, the impact is hard enough to send me flying forward. I smack right into Carrie Hughes, who cries out and tries to grab her back. I know it hurts badly. My body was like a missile launched out of a rocket right into her. Carrie's sobbing like a three-year-old, and all eyes are on me.

I turn extra hot under my two sweaters and T-shirt. A red haze tints my view of Mr. Lux, who's finally turned around.

He's staring right into my eyes. *Zillael, remain calm.*

I'm sure I heard him say that. The words match his expression.

"Oops, sorry." Riley giggles.

I'm still clutching the sides of the desk. My fingers dig into the hard, dried-up gum stuck underneath the tabletop.

Do not hurt her, he says again.

Because I'm so bewildered, the red haze disappears. The anger subsides. Carrie is escorted to the nurse's office. The bell buzzes.

At first, nobody moves. Eyes are still on me and Mr. Lux, staring at each other.

He looks away to say, "Finish Chapter Three tonight."

I rush out the door, happy that this is the final class of the day. I never linger when it's time to go home. The campus gives me the heebie-jeebies, but this is my final year. One day I won't have to walk through the gray-and-tan laminate floors that are never quite clean enough. I won't have to see another tin locker or be forced to read all those flyers urging students to be in this club or attend that event. I'm in no club. I attend zero events.

I'm almost out the front door and into the bitter cold when I hear, "Miss Decker."

I heave a deep, exasperated sigh because I already know who's calling me. "What?"

I turn around to see Mrs. Lowenstein, the guidance counselor, shuffling toward me in her tight black patent leather heels. How many times have I heard the sound of her tiny little feet moving toward me? Each time, all I want to do is run in the opposite direction. She moves so quickly, and now her little dainty face is only a couple of feet away from mine.

"We'll be seeing you tonight and on time." She's actually asking, but it doesn't sound that way.

"Who's we?" I say, short on patience. Her ability to come off as patronizing each and every time she opens her mouth must be a gift.

She just looks at me with a tight-lipped smile, her way of saying, "I'm not stooping to your level, Miss Decker." I think she calls me that because she can't say Zillael without flubbing it.

I twist my wrist to check the time on my watch. "Well, it doesn't matter because I can't go tonight. Family plans."

She doesn't even begin to wipe away that annoying grin of hers. "Okay. Then I'll call your mother and explain how we—you and I—agreed to have you set up and work the Sadie Hawkins Dance in exchange for missing three days of homeroom last week."

"Yeah, about that. How about we find another punishment? Maybe something that makes more sense? I can stay after school and bang erasers or something."

That smile of hers gets even more smug, which I didn't think was possible. "You're definitely a charming one, Miss Decker. You should use your powers for good."

That's even more annoying than her tight-lipped grin.

"As opposed to what?" I ask. Can't help it; even I know I'm a sarcastic smart aleck.

In response, Mrs. Lowenstein spins around on her heels. "Seven thirty." She walks in the opposite direction, unruffled and cooler than the snowy day.

As she walks away, my jaw still drops. I'm left speechless. Then I realize everyone around me is staring. They must have overheard everything. Only in a small town like this would anyone care to listen to a guidance counselor press a student into going to a stupid dance. I glare at their nosy faces, shake my head, and stumble out into the cold.

CHAPTER

TWO

I live three miles from the school, but I walk to and from, even when the snow is over three feet deep. I like walking because I've always been able to do it way faster than the average person. I run really fast too.

In sixth grade, we were required to run a mile. It took me two minutes to get it done, which shocked the dickens out of the gym teacher. She called Deanna, my mother, into the principal's office. I remember sitting in a big, scarlet, squishy leather chair, keeping my eyes on my hands, which were folded in my lap. Deanna argued that running too fast wasn't grounds for a meeting with the principal.

Deanna pulled me out of that school the same

day, enrolled me in my first private school, and warned me to make sure I'm always second to cross the finish line. That was it.

That's what I do for the first mile of my walk home—make sure I keep pace with the fastest person walking in the recently released pack of students. Finding that person is hard to do today because a peculiar fog, which wasn't there when Mrs. Lowenstein stopped me, has just touched down.

The vapor is smothering, and I can hardly see a few feet around me. Those students who are rolling out of the parking lot are moving so slowly they might as well park and walk with me.

I hear a "Hey," and I turn to my left. The one and only Derek Firth is walking beside me.

I don't say anything. I pick up my pace, intending to leave him in the dust. I'm confident that no one can keep up with me, not even him. And he's captain of the hockey team and basketball team. I heard from Riley, during one of her many conversations with Morgan behind me in physics, that he's joined the football team too.

When I'm out of his sight, he shouts, "What's your problem with me anyway, Zillael?"

I'm always running away from him. I think it's

because, like all the other guys in school, he stares at me all the time. I'm not delusional. I understand Riley's problem with me. Even I'm intimidated by the chick staring back at me in the mirror. She and I have nothing in common. Her silky long black hair, almost yellow eyes, and delicate golden skin is not who I am on the inside.

I stop in my tracks today because his little girlfriend kicked the back of my chair one too many times earlier, and *that's* what we need to discuss.

"Listen." I turn to face him, but I can barely see him. My feet had carried me pretty far from him. After a few steps toward each other, we stand face to face.

"Listen," I say again, assuming he didn't hear me the first time.

"I'm listening," he says.

"Tell your little girlfriend to back off, or she's going to get herself hurt pretty bad."

He blurts a chuckle. "What girlfriend?"

"You *know* who I'm talking about."

"I don't have a girlfriend, Zillael."

We stand there staring at each other. My eyes narrow. A group of girls pass and give me the evil eye. It seems like every single chick in the school looks out for Riley, which baffles me because she's such a nasty, self-centered witch. How could she have allies? What's even worse is that even though I want to punch her out, something deep inside of me empathizes with her. I can actually explain how society made her into a poor fractured girl who thinks beauty is so valuable she has to conquer and dominate to feel worthy. But today, she almost got herself killed—*yes, I could've killed her*—and that bothers me.

"Okay, well, whatever Riley thinks she is to you, she's taking it out on me because she knows you like me."

He chuckles. "Who said I like you?"

I step forward to get more up in his face. "Listen, I have no time for games. You know you like me. But here's the deal—I don't like you," I say with a nonchalant shrug."

He laughs even harder, and I frown at him, strangely irritated by his response.

"You know what I've noticed about you?" he asks.

"See, that's what I mean. Why are you noticing things about me?"

He sighs. "Because you're interesting, Zillael, or can I call you Zill?"

I grunt. "Is Zill my name?"

"No."

"Then there's your answer."

He points at me. "That's what I mean. You've taken the word bitch, and I'm not calling you that, but you've taken that noun to a whole other level."

I stare at him, confused. I feel as if I'm having a conversation with Mrs. Lowenstein, and she's managed to call me a bitch without actually calling me a bitch. I'm not buying his reasoning.

"You just called me a bitch," I staunchly conclude.

"But that's not a bad thing. What I meant was you're an unapologetic hardass."

I throw a hand up. "Okay, stop while you're ahead." I walk off. I glance at him with a frown when he easily keeps up with me.

"Come on, you know how you are. All I'm saying is I like it."

I pick up the pace, and he still keeps up. "What do you want from me, Firth?" My tone is harsh.

"I heard you have to go to the Sadie Hawkins dance, and I was wondering if you had asked anyone."

I come to an abrupt stop and grab the collar of his dark gray pea coat. His eyes are a pure dark green. *Strange.* "What are you and your little girl-friend trying to pull? A Carrie?"

"Carrie who?" He looks confused.

"You know the movie *Carrie*? Because I'm telling you, I'll hurt both of you."

"I told you, Riley's not my girlfriend."

"Then why does everyone think she is?"

"I don't know. Maybe because she kissed me in the cafeteria once."

I shake my head. That is the most asinine reason I ever heard. "See what I mean? You're lying to me." I take off again.

"No, I'm not," he says.

"Listen, I don't have a date. Don't want a date." I increase my pace, but he still manages to keep up.

"So you're going alone."

"Didn't the gossipers tell you I'm being punished? I'm working off my time."

"Okay, well, I'll work off time with you."

I shake my head. "Leave me alone, *kid*," I say in my attempt to make a clear distinction between him and me. Although I'm in high school—and man, I hate high school—I'm taller and more filled out than just about everyone. I've physically outgrown this place, and the schoolwork is monotonous.

"You're referring to me as a kid?" He grins and seems pretty amused, but I don't care.

"Yes, now go away!"

That's when he stops, and I keep walking. "See you tonight," I hear him shout.

I shake my head and continue making my way home. The fog is thick but not panic-worthy. This is Moonridge, Maine, a tiny port town along the Atlantic coastline. We're used to fog, but the mist normally rolls in early in the morning or at night, and never this dense.

I know I'm passing the Tackle Barn bait shop, Krispy's Café, and the only McDonald's in town. I enter our shallow downtown, where the structures are barely visible from the sidewalk. I know I'm passing the mayor's symbols of progress, which are two glass buildings designed by Rodale Washington. The only reason I remember the guy's name is because for about a year prior to the grandiose ground-breaking ceremony, posters were plastered on every light post and in every shop window in town. Not only that, but a cheesy billboard was erected at the site of construction, featuring the architect smiling like the guy who just sold our Mr. Mayor muddy swampland for a few million bucks.

Rodale   Washington—Architect   of   the   Century—

Building Moonridge into the 21st Century. I thought it sounded awkward; I mean, it said "century" twice. Maybe it should've said *Architect of the Decade.* Just saying…

What's really funny is my mom, Deanna Decker, couldn't recall seeing even one of those posters or the humongous billboard. She only took notice after seeing the actual buildings while driving up Main Street in that red convertible Corvette of hers. She'd just returned from an extended business trip to California, then New York, then Denver, then Seattle, and then finally here. My mom lives on the road, taking first-class flights to five-star hotels. As far as I'm concerned, she hasn't suffered long enough in this place to call it home.

Yet even with the glass towers, which look completely forced into existence, the town's pride and joy are the quaint cottage-styled shops that form the Main Street Towne Square.

Once I pass downtown, I continue up Main Street for about another mile. I'm relieved to see our mailbox. The fog is starting to wear on me. It's not the regular wet kind that flows off the ocean. The haze is dry and unnaturally cold. Not only that, but it's seriously unsettling.

THREE

I t's toasty inside the house. The iciness has kicked on the central heating system, and it's been blowing all day. I drop my full book bag on the armchair near the front door and call for no one. Deanna's on another long business trip. She checks in every day to make sure I've done the shopping, cooked dinner, and gotten to bed on time. That must make her feel more like a mother.

I turn on the television. The news isn't reporting what the fog may be, so I turn it off. I'm not a big TV watcher. I go into the kitchen and put together a spring salad for dinner. I'm still debating on whether to show up for the dance or not. It's foggy outside, for goodness' sake. Surely that's enough to cancel a silly dance.

After chopping the tomatoes and cucumbers, I shuffle over to the telephone to call the school's office. It rings before I can lift the receiver. It's five thirty, so I know who's calling.

"Hi, Mom," I say right away.

"You're home," Deanna says through a hard sigh of relief.

"Of course, where else can I go? This place sucks."

"Yes, yes..." She's being dismissive, and it makes me mad.

"Plus, this creepy thick fog rolled in and—"

"What fog?" Her tone is completely different, as though she's about to miraculously take whatever I say seriously.

I hesitate, debating whether to take the opportunity to voice how much I hate Moonridge and how unfair it is for her to traipse off to the exciting parts of the world without me. "Fog-fog," I decide to answer instead.

"Isn't it kind of early for fog?"

"Yeah." I think I'm pouting a little because we're not discussing ways to get me out of Moonridge forever.

After a long pause she asks, "How does it feel?"

"What do you mean by *feel*?"

"When you're in it, how does it feel on your skin?"

I frown. "I don't know—like fog. Although it *is* colder and sort of dry." There's long pause. I can feel heaviness in the silence. "Mom, are you there?"

"Yes," she barely says.

"Are you okay?" Now I'm worried about her.

"Listen, Z-cup, stay inside. Don't go out for anything, not even if the yard is on fire. Understand?"

She called me *Z-cup*. She only does that when she wants me to feel comforted.

"Sure, Mom," I haphazardly agree. Except I do have the issue of the dance. All I need is for Lowenstein to call Deanna and tell her I missed homeroom three times last week.

When Mr. Pratt, our principal, had asked me why I'd missed class, all I could come up with was the truth: homeroom is a gross waste of time. I think my answer and the nonchalant way I said it really worried him. He sent me to see Lowenstein right away. After asking me a multitude of questions about friends, of which I have none, and activities I'm involved in, which again added up to zero, she imparted the punishment of me having to work every school event for the next three months.

"That's almost the rest of the school year," I cried.

"I know," she said and stretched her lips into that smile I hate.

Of course, I could blow tonight off and fight the sentence. I could use my grades as evidence that I'm doing all right in school. Missing homeroom doesn't affect them. My grade-point average is above four point zero, but words like "missing class" and "punishment" are hot-button words to my mother. She goes way overboard. Then before I know it, Aunt Jill, a long-time nanny who really isn't my aunt, will knock on the door to announce she's come to—exact words—"babysit" me. And that's an entirely different situation.

Before hanging up, Deanna assures me she'll be home as soon as possible. She's in Sydney, but she's taking the first flight out. When I ask if she's coming back because of the fog, she just hangs up.

I move forward with my plan to call the school. One of the ladies in the office tells me the dance is still on.

"Great," I grumble and hang up.

There's no way I'm going to be AWOL. After I eat my salad, I sit down to read the chapters Mr. Lux assigned and then finish up my trigonometry homework. It takes all of an hour and a half. I'm also assigned to read *The Tempest* by Shakespeare and Chapter Sixteen in my world geology text, but I read them in the first two weeks of the new school year. I'd figured why not get a jump on it all because if I could hurry up and get it done, then maybe that would speed up the process of finishing high school. *I guess it didn't work.*

At seven thirty, I throw on an old pair of loose-fitting jeans and a white T-shirt under a navy blue cable-knit sweater. The goal is to look like the help and not a partygoer. I don't know what to do with my hair. Ponytails and tie-ups are out of the question; they're too binding. I need to be free, always free. Even I admit I look too much like a walking Calvin Klein ad with my hair down. I need to blend in, go unnoticed. I wonder when or if that day will ever come. Regardless of how I look, time is ticking away, so I grab my green wool winter coat and hit the door.

When I get outside, I see the fog has lifted. The sky is congested with gloomy clouds. It's extra dark, which makes Moonridge look even more like one of those tiny deserted towns on the edge of nowhere. I don't want to walk tonight because it's just too depressing.

Deanna bought me a black Jeep Wrangler with black tinted windows that I mostly drive only to Whole Foods in Portland. I'll take it tonight because I want to feel like I'm traveling far away and not pulling double duty at high school.

FOUR

T he parking lot is crowded. Only in a town like this will an event like the Sadie Hawkins dance be over-attended. I park in the faculty lot because it's emptier and the plow did a better job clearing out the snow.

The students filtering in to the auditorium are all dressed up. Some of the girls, who have forgone their coats, are hugging themselves while stomping into the building as fast as they can. I shake my head, wondering, *Why the sacrifice?*

I check my watch. It's eight thirty. Great, I'm late. After taking a deep breath, I shuffle across the icy asphalt. Once I mix into the crowd, just about everyone stares at me. I think they're shocked to see me. I keep my face down and weave through the bystanders until I make it to the front door.

"Ticket," a little pointy-faced girl asks. I see her bottom lip tremble. She's not wearing a coat even though she's sitting at the table taking tickets.

"Don't have one. But I have to go in," I say, half hoping she'll refuse me. That way, I can tell Mrs. Lowenstein tomorrow that I came, but the commando manning the door wouldn't let me in.

Then I hear those little shoes tap, tap, tap, and I look through the open doorway. Here she comes, still wearing her tight suit from earlier. The look on her face makes me sigh. This encounter won't go well.

"Sorry," I say before she's able to get out a word. "Lots going on at home, and I lost track of time."

She sighs. "Well, you're here now. Follow me." She turns and saunters off, expecting me to keep up.

I give the girl manning the door one last glance before following Mrs. Lowenstein. Funny, I've never seen that girl before, or if I have, I don't remember her face—which isn't odd for me. I can't remember more than half of the faces or names of the people in this school, and we've been classmates for the better part of three years. That's how long we've lived here—well, *I've* lived here.

Inside, there's crepe paper and hay everywhere. It's sort of ironic—a one-horse town and barnyard décor. As I pass people, they watch me stride across the glossy wooden floor. It's ridiculous. Shouldn't they focus on those who want to be here, basically each other?

"You could've worn something a little dance-worthy." Mrs. Lowenstein says over her shoulder.

"I'm working, right?"

"Yes, the punch containers."

I easily catch up to her. "The what?"

She stops, so I stop too. "The punch, Miss Decker."

"That's my punishment? Serve punch to kids?"

"Do you mean your peers?"

"Okay," I say haughtily, "peers."

"Chop, chop, the *kids* are getting thirsty," she says before walking off.

I look at the table with cupcakes, cookies, and all sorts of candies for sale. Then there's the punch dispenser with Derek Firth standing right next to it and grinning at me.

"Great," I say to myself and reluctantly walk off to take my post. I thought I'd be moving tables and chairs, setting up speakers or something, not serving refreshments.

FIVE

"See, I'm your date for tonight after all," Derek whispers in my ear.

I step away from him. "What are you doing here?"

"Volunteering." He's still grinning.

I snort. "You should stop. Really."

I search the floor and find Riley grouped with about four other girls, beaming in on us.

"You want me to stop volunteering?"

"You know what I'm talking about."

A spikey-haired kid steps up to the punch containers. "Need a cup," he says to me.

I pick up a waxy cardboard cup, put it under the spout, pull the knob, and fill it. "Here you go." When I look past him, I see a whole line of people has formed. "He's serving too." I shove a cup toward Derek and stab a finger in his direction, telling the next kid to go there.

"So you *do* want me to volunteer?" Derek asks through a snarky grin.

"I guess." I keep my eyes on my task as I serve the next person.

"Two lines," he says. He's not even close to sounding as odious as I did, and the students reluctantly split. "See, I'm not the only one who finds you interesting," Derek whispers too close to my ear.

I glance at the line of partygoers who are all looking at me. "That's because you're all hicks."

"Ha, so that's what you think of the local color?"

I pour and hand out the next drink while thinking about what Derek just asked me. Sure, he's being funny, but my answer is full of rage. Not toward him. He's just a conduit for what really irks me.

From sixth to ninth grade, I attended an all-girl's private school in Manhattan, where being a loner was much easier. I hated the way I looked in that blue coat and little gray skirt with knee-high socks because almost every guy I passed would stare at me. I knew what I looked like: some rock video chick who's only seconds away from tearing out of the naughty schoolgirl uniform. Even when I wore a longer skirt and baggier coat, they stared. The girls at school paid me no attention for the most part. There were a handful of jealous girls, and we had our run-ins.

But the social structure in public school has been so jolting that I've turned bitter toward the entire institution and the town. I want out. I want far away from here. Yet I don't want to hate anyone or anything in the meantime, and unfortunately, I do.

"No, they're not all hicks, I guess." That was a mean thing to say, and although I'm grouchy a lot, I try not to be a mean person.

"I know you're not mean. Just moody," he says.

He and I lock eyes. I want to hold onto the way he said that, the tone of his voice. I didn't say that out loud. He couldn't have heard my thoughts— could he?

"Excuse me." Derek and I step back from each other, and Riley stands in front of me saying, "Punch, punch girl."

I fill up a cup and shove it at her. "Here you go."

She doesn't take it. "Did you two come together?" Her eyes dance between me and Derek.

"No, we didn't," Derek says.

"Oh. Because if you did then…"

We're both watching her, waiting for the rest.

"Well, just…then." Without taking the cup, she cuts in front of the person standing before Derek and leans toward him. "Um, can we talk?"

That's when I stop paying attention. Derek steps off to oblige Riley's request, leaving me there all alone. A seriously mundane pop tune is playing. Couples dance together by shifting back and forth. Some girls dance with girls to keep from being bored. The boys who showed up without being asked are holding up the walls. Most are standing in groups, clutching their cups of punch, and talking. It looks like no one is having that much fun.

After a short while, no one is standing in front of me waiting for punch. The dim lights and general boredom makes me yawn. Then I hear those little heels go click, click. I turn, and there's Mrs. Lowenstein, wearing that tight-lipped grin.

"You should go to the kitchen and make another batch."

I blink, taken aback. "Me, make punch?"

"It's just water and sugary syrup," says Mrs. Sarcastic.

"So where am I supposed to go? To the cafeteria?"

"The front doors are open, and the light is on in the kitchen. You'll find the mix on the counter." She scans the auditorium. "You may want to ask Mr. Firth to assist you. Where is he anyway?"

Probably behind the building playing tongue hockey with his deranged girlfriend, who he insists is not his girlfriend. I'm pretty sure Mrs. Lowenstein isn't looking for an answer. Her heels tap away from me when she sees two guys pulling the "SADIE" paper banner off the wall.

I snatch the plastic container off the table and stomp across the floor and out into the icy night.

CHAPTER

SIX

S now flurries are falling. It's still and quiet, so the peace of being away from the pop music and teenagers soothes me. I carry the container up the walk to the cafeteria. Nothing moves around the flat block buildings that line the path. I shuffle up the steps to the next level.

Strange, but I halfway expected to find Derek and Riley making out somewhere between the buildings. That causes me to feel a grave feeling that is unexpected and unwanted. This guy can't be getting to me. Nothing about this town appeals to me, not even the boys, no matter how good looking one may be. I'm forced to admit that Derek Firth is attractive, and he's luring me into him by piquing my interest.

The cafeteria is just as Mrs. Lowenstein said it would be. The lights are on, and the doors are unlocked. The sounds of my thick-heeled, black leather hiking boots smashing against the linoleum replaces the normal chatter. The scene is what teen horror flicks are made of. I almost expect Jason or Freddy Krueger to sneak up behind me with an axe. I glance over my shoulder to make sure that's not about to happen.

I walk through the metal, swinging double doors into the kitchen. I see the red syrup on the counter in a plastic container. I go to work twisting the cap off the punch dispenser, pouring a portion of the red liquid into it, and walking it over to the industrial-sized sink.

As the water runs, I think about Deanna's warning. The fog is long gone, so I'm sure she's calmed down and canceled her flight home. Although I hope she didn't. It's time for her to do some time in Moonridge. She hasn't stayed her a full two weeks in three years. I truly believe that after one month without her posh, cosmopolitan perks, she'll come to her senses. We'll be packed and back in Manhattan in less than two days.

I'm simpering over the joys of that possibility when, out of nowhere, there's a loud *bang*. I jump, startled. My eyes search the kitchen, trying to figure out where the sound came from. Now there's a constant scratching. I turn the faucet off to hear it better. I stand still, listening. It *is* scratching, interrupted by intermittent, faint knocking.

Down past the stainless steel industrial-sized refrigerators, there's a door. That's where the scratching is coming from. I tiptoe toward it. My heart knocks against my chest. There's another loud bang, and I jump. Then there's nothing.

I know what I'm capable of. Most girls would run away as fast as they could and seek help, but me? I *am* the help. My ears remain on high alert as I move toward the door, carefully twist the bolts, turn the doorknob, and pull the door open.

I'm instantly hit by freezing air. I look up and down the narrow walk outside, but I don't see anything. Then I look down. A red substance on the ground is starting to freeze. I squat and run a finger through the slushy fluid. *Is it blood?* Just as I examine my find, I feel a presence. I look up to see three big guys glaring at me. I'm stunned, frozen in place. Though I'm scared out of my mind, my instincts tell me to fake bravery.

"Hey," I say as I rise cautiously.

Upon study, it's my guess that these guys are

definitely not from around here. They're wearing crisp, high-end jeans, the sort the trendy boys in Manhattan wear when they go clubbing. Their haircuts are sleek. What I notice most is that they're not wearing coats, and they don't look the least bit cold.

"Wow. Look at her," one says to the other.

"Do you smell that?" the other one asks.

They all sniff the air like animals and look at me with gleaming eyes. I study the contours of their faces. They have an anemic, olive-skin complexion and shallow beards. They're good looking, but there's something menacing about them.

"Found her," the first guy says.

"Told she was one of them," the third guys says.

I wait to hear what I am, but they all just stare at me as if I'm dinner or something. The look on their faces energizes every muscle in my body. I'm ready for them.

Then I hear another bang. My instincts are on high alert, so I don't take my eyes off the three guys. The first one rushes me, but what's in me takes over. I shift to the right clamp both of my hands around his torso, pick him up, and throw him like a bowling ball into the other two. They all hit the snow. I plant my feet, standing my ground. My fists are balled. Although I can't believe this is happening, I'm in the thick of it, and the only way out is to fight and win.

As the men find their footing, I glance down by the dumpster and see someone's legs in the dark crevice between the large green container and the wall of the building. I turn back to face my opponents.

All three of them charge me, and I go on automatic kick ass. There's no training behind my movements. My limbs respond instinctively, and I'm strong. The guys are matching me blow for blow—and that's really strange. I hit them, and they come back as if I'm having no effect at all.

I don't want to hurt them too badly, but I know they're not schoolyard bullies. When one of them kicks at my head, I know the intent behind that blow. If it had connected, I'd be hurt badly. It would take more than that to kill me though. My right hand catches his foot, and I throw him at least fifty feet. Soon after, my left elbow cracks another one in the neck hard enough to send him to the ground clutching his throat and gasping until he's out cold. *One down, two to go*. I have no time to assess what my next move should be. These guys are not giving up.

Just when I'm ready to maim the other two, a white flash shoots through the air. Right before my eyes, the two would-be aggressors lay face down in the snow. Their bodies are twisted and mangled. Derek Firth stands right beside me, glaring down at his kills.

"What? How…" I can barely squeeze words through my voice box.

Derek squats beside one of them, flips him over, and pulls open his mouth. He puts his finger on the guy's teeth.

"Selells." Derek frowns as he stands. "But there's something different about these creatures."

I'm blinking like crazy, wondering if what just happened really just happened. "What did you call these guys?"

"These are Selells." Derek seems distracted. He looks over by the dumpster. "There's another one."

He goes over, grabs the guy's leg, and pulls him out of his hiding place. I gasp, shocked at first.

There's a seriously deep gash in his neck and blood is just pouring out of it.

"Is he alive?" I ask, craning my head forward, hoping to see something that looked more logical.

"Not really," Derek mutters, keeping his eyes on the injured party.

"He's dead?" I look at the other three bodies lying around us like road kill. "Are they all dead?"

"Those three are gone. This one isn't—yet."

"What do you mean by yet?" I freaked out. I hope Derek isn't planning on killing him. "Maybe it's a good time to call the cops."

Derek looks up at me. Why does he look so calm when I'm freaking out? Then the guy on the ground groans.

"These are not human beings, Zillael. Deep down, you know that. So help me," he says, more like orders.

I move swiftly to shield the guy with my body.

"No!" Derek snatches me away from the guy.

I fly about ten feet through the air, but I land solidly on my feet. Normally, I would try to hide the fact that I can do that, but something tells me I don't have to keep this part of me from Derek Firth.

"What is wrong with you?" I yell at him.

"Stay away from him." He uses himself as a

wall between me and the injured boy, whose face I haven't seen yet.

"Is he a student or something? I'm not going to get freaked out if that's what you're worried about."

"He's not a student here."

"Fine, but I know I can save him." I try to make another move toward the injured boy, but Derek blocks me.

"Can't let you," he says while holding my shoulders.

I frown at him. "Move." I try to push him, but he stands solid.

"He's a Selell."

"A what? What's that?"

He hesitates. "If you don't know what that means, then I can't tell you."

"You're making zero sense," I say as I look down.

The guy is crawling deeper into the crevice. That's good news. If I weren't sure of Derek's intention to kill him, then I would say something. All I know is that there's a life to preserve, Selell or not. I shift without warning to shake Derek and dive to the ground, landing between the wall and the guy. He and I face each other.

I take his hand. "Does it hurt?"

Derek stands over us, blocking the light.

"Not anymore," the wounded boy whispers. His eyes are coal black and sincere. His skin matches the white of the snow his cheek rests on. His hair is as black as mine, and he has a dark, warrior look that's probably passé.

I don't know why, but my fingers lightly stroke the soft skin of his straight forehead. More is happening between us. It's freezing cold, but I'm engulfed by warmth from the moment I touch him. I look up at Derek, who's watching us, stunned.

"We're going to have to get help," I say.

Then, to my utter shock, Mr. Lux appears behind Derek as if he just dropped out of the sky.

EIGHT

"Mr. Lux?" I'm happy to see him. Finally, the guy's going to be safe; authority has arrived. Then I notice that Mr. Lux's blue eyes are glowing like light bulbs.

"The three behind us," Derek says after a quick glance over his shoulder.

I see something long and on fire in Mr. Lux's hand. Maybe it's a sword of some sort. Curious about what he's going to do, I shuffle to my feet. When the guy and I stop touching, I don't get cold again. My eyes don't deceive me. Mr. Lux slices through the Selells on the ground, and one by one, they turn into ashes. My mouth opens in disbelief. Mr. Lux doesn't intend to stop there. He puts those intense blue eyes on the guy lying by the dumpster.

I want to shout stop, but I only have time to form the "s." The Selell, as Derek calls him, flips onto his feet so quickly that I'm sure my eyes are playing tricks on me. As Mr. Lux lowers his fire beam at him, the guy flips backward, avoiding the blade, and flips again before he's gone.

"I've never seen anybody move that fast, Lux," Derek says as if they're old friends and not teacher and student.

"I'll catch him," Mr. Lux declares.

"No," I say. "Don't." I'm quite confused, of course, and Mr. Lux glares at me as though I've done something very naughty.

"It was Zillael," he says, stabbing me with those ice blue eyes. "You gave him power."

"Me?" Now I'm really confused.

"Do you think they're bonded, and that's why he's here?" Derek asks.

"It's happened with another Life Blood."

They both look at me.

"When you say Life Blood, do you mean me?" I ask.

Derek and Mr. Lux look at each other as if, for the first time, they realize I'm actually present.

"Get her back inside." Mr. Lux says and shoots away faster than humanly possible.

Derek and I stand alone in the purple night behind the cafeteria. It's as if reality reset itself, and none of what just happened ever happened. Three boys run across the field next to campus. They're throwing snowballs at each other and laughing loudly. To them, life is normal. Funny, but I think I finally feel the same way. Derek studies my distant expression.

"What about all the blood?" I say, putting myself back in the moment.

"It's gone."

"What?" I study the ground where the guy bled, and what was once blood has turned into a black tar-like substance.

Then I look at my fingers where I touched the blood earlier—again, black tar. Derek and I just stare at each other. I'm trying to fully absorb the moment and him in it. Then I remember I have a job to do.

"I guess I should get that punch back down to the auditorium," is all I can think to say in the moment.

"This was never supposed to happen," he says.

"It's okay. I guess."

Again, he's just staring into my face. I've never really looked at him before. He's a lot like me in the sense that he doesn't look like he belongs in high school.

I thumb toward the door. "I'll go now. We'll talk later?"

After a long pause, he nods. I go inside, and he stays outside. The container filled with red liquid is exactly where I left it. I scrub the tar off my hand and then take the container by the handles and lift it out of the sink. It's as light as a pail of straw.

When I get back to the dance, nothing's changed. The boys are still holding up the walls. More girls are dancing with each other than with someone of the opposite sex. The music still sucks. No one's standing around the refreshment table waiting for punch. The girl with the short haircut who was working the table at the entrance has taken over serving.

"Where have you been?" she scolds as I plop the container on the tabletop.

"Busy, as you can see."

She stares at me—more precisely, at my cheek. "Did you get into a fight?" She sounds a little miffed that the task took me so long.

"Why?" I touch the spot her eyes beam in on and wince a little. It's tender. I guess I caught one in the face without even feeling it.

"Who did you fight? Riley?" Her eyes are shining.

"No, it was three guys," I say, knowing she'll never believe me.

"Three guys—who?"

"Tweedledee, Tweedledum and Frick without Frack."

She rolls her eyes. "You're such a bitch."

"That's a pretty brave thing to say to a chick who just creamed three guys." I look at her with a crazy grin.

She grunts. "Handle it, I'm done."

Of course, as soon as she stomps away, another little mousy-faced girl steps up for a cup of punch. As I'm filling the cup, I see Mr. Lux and Mrs. Lowenstein walk into the auditorium. He's saying something to her. She nods once and heads toward me. I look down when I hear punch spatter on the floor.

"Shoot," I curse under my breath.

I hand the girl the overfilled cup, and she takes it. "Sorry about that," she says.

I'm caught off guard. That was actually nice.

"They're not all bad," Derek says right behind me.

Before I can turn to reply, Mrs. Lowenstein is

standing in front of me without that condescending smile, she usually wears when talking to me. "You can leave now. We're all settled up on your sentence."

I watch her walk away. I don't know what Mr. Lux said to her, but I'm sure that's the reason she released me from an entire year of social event hell.

"Go," Derek says as he steps up beside me. "I'll finish up here."

I swallow hard. Heck, I don't have to be told twice. Without looking at him, I trek across the high gloss floor. I slow down when Morgan Slater runs to catch up to me.

"Um, Riley wants to talk to you," she says as if the queen has spoken and I should know to bow and comply.

Unfortunately for her, my deep-embedded senses are heightened from the fight. "Move." I barely shove her out of my way, but she goes tumbling to the floor. I keep walking. I'll deal with the fallout tomorrow.

A black car with black tinted windows, too *chichi* for this town, follows me from the faculty parking lot all the way to our driveway. Once I make the right onto our property, it slows and stops along the side of the road. I'm a little nervous. Maybe whoever's in there is a friend of the three "Selells." That's what Derek calls them.

I hit the button to open the garage, drive in, and hit the quick drop safety button. The garage door closes with a dead drop. Deanna had the mechanism installed the day after we moved in. I'd thought it was a waste of money because, really, who's going to rob us in this one-horse town? Nobody that I couldn't take down in five seconds. However, tonight's fight cured me of being over-confident.

Once safely confined, I sit in the driver's seat and wait for about fifteen minutes. I notice the rake, shovel, and step ladder along one wall, the lawn-mower in the corner on the other side, and a table with bottled water, toilet paper, cleaning supplies, and paper towels against the wall in front of me. From where I sit, it looks like real people live here. An ordinary family without a daughter who can fight like a supercharged Bruce Lee.

It's time to blow this joint. I rush to the side door of the garage and hurry out, searching the road. The car is still there. I fish my house keys out of my coat pocket and run to the front door. I unlock it as fast as I can and lock myself inside. I pull the curtain to gaze out the window; the car is gone.

I waste no time stripping out of my clothes and crawling in bed. But I can't fall asleep. I lay in the dark staring up at the ceiling, unable to fully process my evening. There's a reaction that's evading me.

Let's see…Derek Firth finished off the two guys and showed me the sharp-fanged teeth in their mouths. Mr. Lux carries a fire sword, and that sword turned them into ashes. Then there was the boy, maybe man. He looked to be in his early twenties, but so do I, and I'm seventeen. This *person* with his black eyes, black hair, and wintery complexion lies on the ground injured. Then the next thing I know, he's evading Mr. Lux's sword, and he's out of there. Later, the guy's blood turns into tar.

What's Life Blood? What's a Selell? And what was never supposed to happen?

THE WEK

NINE

The alarm blares, and I slap it until it's off. I open one eye to read the time. The orange LED lights say it's seven thirty. School starts at eight fifteen. It never takes me more than twenty minutes to get dressed and ready. I never wear makeup, and I pretty much don't try to get gussied up in the clothes department either. After last night, I'm tempted to change my attitude against adorning myself for the male eye, which sort of scares me.

I drag myself to the bathroom and look in the mirror. That red bruise is still on my left cheek under my eye. I'm not ready for the stares and the possibility of having to explain what happened to Mrs. Lowenstein—*gosh, she irritates me.*

However, I do want to see Derek Firth. Like he said, we have a lot to discuss. I don't want to deal with Riley Simms, who's always lurking in his shadow. I swear she has some sort of fatal attraction. Either he's leading her on or lying to me or maybe both, which appears to be inconsistent with who I believe he is as a person.

As I inspect myself in my powder blue tank top and pink and blue flannel night pants, a bruise on my face and hair all over the place, it dawns on me that a person who looks and feels like me ought to take a sick day. Without delay, I march right back to my bedroom, climb under the comforter, and fall asleep again.

It seems as soon as I close my eyes, the doorbell chimes. Even after I sit up to focus, the doorbell is still singing that irritating song. Aunt Jill is the only guest we've ever received, and usually Deanna or I open the door for her as soon as we see the cab pull up. So whoever the visitor is, he or she must be a real stranger. I glance at the clock. It's a little after noon. It appears I've been asleep for some time. My head is woozy, and I drag to the door.

"Who is it?" I shout past the frog in my throat.

"It's me."

"Who's me?"

"Derek."

TEN

I almost didn't believe it was him until I opened the door.

He's grinning at me.

"Hey," he says, seemingly glowing under the sooty white sky, which holds a thick layer of snow clouds.

"Hey," I say back.

We stare at each other. I suspect he's waiting for me to say more. "Played hooky."

He studies the bruise on my cheek. "How's that feeling?"

I touch my face. "Okay, I guess. It doesn't hurt. Stuff like this doesn't stay with me long, so… It'll probably be gone tomorrow."

He nods stiffly. "Good," he says, sounding almost overly enthusiastic.

Again, we stare at each other. It's time to change the subject.

"Are you up?" he asks. His eyes fall over me.

"Well, now I am, thanks to you," I say with an over-exaggerated straight face.

He chuckles, which I take to mean I don't have to let him know that was me joking. "So do you want to hang out? You know, in town?"

If he'd asked me that before last night, my answer would've been a firm no. But Derek has a lot to explain. So, instead, I say, "Sure."

I THROW on a pair of oversized overalls, totally forgetting that I'd wanted to appeal to him. Seeking comfort is automatic to me. Some people cram ice cream and cupcakes down their throat for comfort; I throw on something baggy and mundane.

My black boots squash the snow as we walk up the road. I've taken this walk so many times but always alone. Unfortunately, I don't know how to make small talk. I notice the wiry winter branches on the trees in the fields that separate the properties. They make it look as though we all live on our personal New England island.

"Beautiful, huh?" Derek asks.

Now that I'm looking at him, I realize my eyes haven't focused on him since we started walking. "Kind of, I guess."

He grins at me. "You're just not going to give in, are you?"

"Give in to what?"

"To how great it is to live in a place like this."

"Great for whom?"

"You, Zillael."

I love the way he says my name. It's not in the least bit difficult for him, as if he's been saying it his entire life. I'm simpering a bit. That's embarrassing enough for me to change the subject.

"So what's a Selell?" I ask. I figure now is a good time to get to the core of why we're sharing this time together.

"You touched one."

"The guy on the ground? He had canine teeth too?"

"He did."

"So a Selell is a guy with teeth like an animal?" I ask.

"You already know what they are, Zillael. You just don't want to believe it."

I look down to watch my feet squash the snow. A driver of a red truck honks. Derek waves at him.

"You know who that is too?" I ask, surprised. The guy looked older than sixty.

"Mr. Patterson. He's your neighbor."

"Oh." I watch the tail end of the truck continue down the ice-covered road.

"But getting back to the subject, come on, what do you think those guys are? You can say it. I won't laugh or call you crazy."

I swallow hard. I feel ridiculous even knowing what I'm thinking. "Something like a vampire." Doubt colors my tone.

"Wasn't hard, was it?" He grins at me again.

"Yeah, it was."

He laughs.

"You're telling me vampires exist?"

"Selells do, and they're like vampires."

"In what way?"

"Direct sunlight kills them. Blood cures their eternal thirst. They once were regular people but—"

"So what does that make you?" I stare at his

extremely attractive face. I can't wait to hear his answer.

"I'm a Wek."

"A what?" I ask with a laugh. I was not expecting him to say that.

"Something like a guardian. But I'm just not a guardian."

"Okay…" I ponder that. "So what are you guarding?"

"You."

That three-letter word hits me like an anvil. "Me? Why me?"

"Do you want to know what the Life Blood is?"

I kick up the snow as I think. It sounds as though he's actually doing me the courtesy of asking before revealing something disturbing. I'm still trying to process the existence of vampires and him being a Wek. "So why Wek?"

"Why not?" he asks with a chuckle.

We're at the edge of town. I see the two glass buildings, out of place but glistening anyhow.

"You know what, never mind," I say. "If Mayor Taylor can justify that, then by golly, you can be a Wek."

He laughs loudly, and I watch him. I can't

believe I made someone laugh. I've never done that before.

He lowers his face to mine. "Sounds like we agree about something."

I'm simpering. I'm embarrassed again.

"Have you ever eaten Jake's Candy Apples?"

I frown as we take a quick right onto the wooden plank walkway that cuts between the two towers. "A candy apple?"

"Of course you haven't. Follow me." He flashes those pearly whites.

WE SHUFFLE past the Cool Cookies Shop and Our Lady Salon, and we enter the store with an array of candy apples displayed on encased shelves in the window. The scent of apples dipped in hard red candy coating is divine. I study the sweet morsels with wide eyes, mesmerized by how tantalizing they look.

"You look like you've never seen one before," he says to me.

"Not in real life," I confess.

"Hey, Jake," Derek calls.

An older, white-haired guy wearing a blue jean

apron steps out from the back. "Is that you, Derek?" Jake shouts too loudly for Derek and me to be the only two people in the toasty shop. He's trying to focus in on both of us, past his extra thick bifocal lenses. He studies me hard. "Is this your girlfriend?"

"She doesn't even want to be friends, Jake," Derek says jokingly. "But I'm going to bribe her with one of your candy apples."

Jake lets out one loud laugh. "Well, I better make it the best one I have because she sure is a pretty gal." He focuses those magnified eyes harder on me. "Like a movie star."

I don't know why, but I find myself grinning at him. I'm not flattered because looks are just looks, but I feel liked. That makes me happy.

Derek buys two candy apples. We sit outside in the nippy afternoon on one of the black iron benches next to Jake's Candy Apples. My fingers are freezing. So are my lips and the tip of my nose. The candy apple tastes like a bit of heaven on earth, and I don't know what's taken me so long to try one.

"You can't do this in New York," Derek says, reminding me that the candy apple and I aren't alone.

"I guess not," I confess. We smile at each other. I like Derek Firth, even if he is a Wek.

"The Life Blood, do you want to know about it?" he asks.

"Do you have it too? Life Blood? I mean, you took those two…"—I'm not yet ready to call them vampires—"guys out pretty easily. That's something I could always do—fight I guess." I whisper the last part.

"Yes, you're strong."

"So you know that about me already?"

"I know everything about you, and no, you're not a Wek. But I can't tell you anything more about the Life Blood unless you really want to know. Do you really want to know about the Life Blood?"

I study my half-eaten candy apple and run my tongue across my back teeth to try to dislodge the sticky pieces. I'm trying to figure out how to put what I'm thinking into words. I'm not afraid of being judged, but I want to be understood. Finally someone is listening to me. "It's just… I know it's serious, and everything's about to change, isn't it?"

"I don't know, Zillael."

"Okay, you can call me Zill." I grin feebly at him.

"I don't know, Zill," he rephrases while grinning

back. "Can't we kind of assume that things have already changed?"

Clips from last night play in my head. "I guess so."

We sit in silence. A bearded man wearing a plaid coat eyes me as he walks by. I think it's because I'm staring at him. I bet his life is normal. He goes home, whips up some lunch, and watches some television. Maybe he discusses his day with his wife at some point.

Then there's a girl named Phoebe Adams, who always wears black and heavy Goth makeup, plodding through the snow as though she has nowhere to go. She beams in on us, but once she figures out who we are, she doesn't pay us any more attention. I always liked Phoebe, how she's present, yet so far away. I bet there are no vampires in her universe. Her body can't go on autopilot and defend her against any and all aggression. So I ponder, deep down, do I want to be Phoebe or, with all that I know about myself and my reality, remain Zillael?

"Tell me about the Life Blood," I say. *I want to be me.*

Derek's eyes flick over to a couple walking toward us. Foot traffic *is* picking up. "Let's walk."

I follow him up Oak Street and through a residential area where weather-beaten houses are dug in between an array of winter-worn trees. This is where most of the kids at school live.

"Do you live over here?" I take in our surroundings. We've lived in Moonridge for three years, but I've never journeyed to this area.

"No, I don't."

I squint at him. There's something about the way he said that. "Do you live in Main Valley like me?"

"Yeah, I live by you."

"Oh…" I'm sure there's a double meaning in his answer, but I choose to leave it alone. We have more pressing matters to discuss. "So tell me, what's this Life Blood stuff?"

"Have you ever heard of the Tree of Life?"

I rack my brain, trying to remember where I've heard that reference.

"How about the Tree of the Knowledge of Good and Evil?"

"Sounds familiar, but I'm coming up blank."

"They're referenced in a few scripts of the world. Some have been discovered by mankind; many haven't."

I glance at him. Just that the way he's speaking is weird. He doesn't sound like a guy who's popular with the girls at school and captain of just about all the sports teams. As I'm thinking about that, it hits me. "The Bible!"

"Yes."

"The…"—I snap my fingers—"Garden of Eden."

"Exactly."

"That stuff isn't true though. Is it?"

He clamps his lips together and looks forward.

"Are you not going to answer that?" I ask.

"That's for me to know and you to figure out. I can't tell you what to believe, but your blood is life to everything that's lost it."

"When you say 'to everything that's lost its life,' do you mean the dead?" I chuckle. That makes no sense. "Because if someone is dead, then they're buried. Unless you're talking about their soul or something."

If last night hadn't happened, I would call Derek Firth a liar and stomp off after telling him to never say another word to me again. But I actually fought the three "Selells." I have the bruise under my eye to prove it.

"Selells are humans who once possessed a soul, but now they're dead," he coolly says. "As you saw, they're not buried. And they have teeth."

"I guess not," I'm forced to confess. All of sudden, and for the first time since last night, I'm afraid. Reality must've set in. I'm shivering and not from the cold. The dank white sky seems to close in on us, and breathing becomes an elusive exercise.

Derek stops to take my shoulders. "I'm not going to tell you that life gets easier from this point on, but I'm here, and so is Lux."

That's right. "Mr. Lux. What the heck is he?"

"He's your protector."

"But I thought you were my protector?"

He takes his hands off my shoulders. "No, I'm your Wek."

"Something like a guardian. So I need a protector and a guardian?" I muse.

Derek is still studying my face. He knows I'm thinking. I like how he takes care to never interrupt that process. Maybe that's what a Wek does.

"So what next?" I ask.

"We have to wait and see."

"I'm okay with that."

"Good."

"Good."

We grin at each other and then head back to my house. Now I know why he can keep up with me. School must've let out. We slow our speed without discussion as we sweep past the first group of curious students and then another and then the final group before heading up Main Street toward the less populated part of town.

"How old are you?" I ask.

"I don't have an age."

"You were never a baby or a child or anything?"

"No, I wasn't."

I just look at him, mystified. He has ten fingers and a nose and a mouth. He ate the candy apple today, so he has teeth and a tongue. Like me, he's definitely a human being. "That doesn't make sense."

"I'm mirroring a human."

"So you're mirroring us?"

"I'm mirroring humans."

I grunt a laugh, convinced he's joking with me again. "Are you saying I'm not a human?"

He shuts his mouth tightly, which I've learned means he's choosing not to elaborate any further. But this conversation is not over for me.

"Am I?" I insist.

After a long moment of silence, he says, "I can't tell you."

"You started it. You shouldn't have mentioned it

if you didn't want to finish it. It's not fair." I'm whining. I hate whining.

"I know," he admits and glances at me. "I'm sure I'm doing this all wrong. I want to tell you everything, Zill, but believe me, I can't."

We're running out of time. I see my house up ahead, a sprawling one-story dwelling that sits far back from the road. For the first time, I see how excessive it looks. It has five bedrooms, four bathrooms, a great room, living room, den, office, dining room, and a humongous kitchen that rarely gets used past making salads, sandwiches, and bowls of cereals for breakfast by me. It's a lot of living space for two people, and one's hardly ever home. The sight of it makes me feel something, and finally I can say what that something is.

"I'm afraid, Derek," I confess and get the chills. "I don't want to be alone."

We stop in front of my house.

"You've never been alone. Just call for me, and I'll be here," he says.

Something tells me he means it.

THE LONER

ELEVEN

The next morning, I'm awakened by the sound of the alarm. As usual, my head is foggy, and I struggle against the urge to curl up and go back to sleep. I mean, I have "Life Blood" and may not be human. Those two facts should excuse me from having to ever show up for high school again. Instead of giving in to what I want, I slide out of bed to prepare for the day.

I rifle through the closet, taking my time to find something a little more than plain. It occurs to me that I'm split between two feelings: hatred of sitting in class all day, especially physics with Riley and Morgan, and excitement at seeing Derek Firth again.

After sleeping on the talk we had yesterday, I feel as though everything I learned about myself was part of a dream and the fight behind the cafeteria a nightmare. None of it feels real any longer. The fear is gone. Life has reset itself, and I think I like it.

I throw on a pair of fitted jeans and my black turtleneck sweater that's fitted too. Once, I'd gone shoe shopping on Fifth Avenue with Deanna. She talked me into buying a pair of patent leather ankle boots with a two-inch heels.

"Live a little," she'd urged me.

So I'd chosen to make her happy and let her buy them for me. After slipping on both shoes, I trot off to Deanna's bedroom to look myself over in the full-length mirror.

"Wow," I whisper. I look like an actual supermodel. I stand there, torn for a moment. Then I remember the deep emerald eyes I kept staring into yesterday and decide to go with it.

I drive the jeep again. I'd feel a bit uncomfortable walking ten miles in the clothes I'm wearing. I'm still questioning whether I made the right decision as I pull into the faculty parking lot. I park at the far back of the lot next to Mr. Cranston's beat-up yellow Hyundai. I know exactly who drives each car; it's part of my strategy.

Mr. Cranston hardly remembers students' names, let alone what we drive. I also park next to Mr. O'Toole, who's a disbarred lawyer and hates being here just as much as I do. He never pays attention to any of us either.

Last year in political science, Bill Lintner had tried to kiss up to him. Mr. O'Toole just got fed up and yelled, "Stop it, you kiss ass!"

Everyone was shocked, but I dropped my head and chuckled. Really, it was about time Bill Lintner heard it, even if it didn't cure him from being a kiss ass. Of course, Mr. O'Toole got reprimanded and had to apologize to Lintner and the entire class. After we were dismissed that day, I walked up to his desk and said, "No need to say sorry to *me*, Mr. O'Toole," and walked out. From that moment on, the few times he's seen me parking in the faculty lot, he pretends I'm invisible.

I slide cautiously out of my car, taking care to go undetected by the teachers.

"Breaking the rules again," I hear right behind me.

I whip around to see the owner of those green

eyes grinning at me. I'm holding my chest. "You scared me."

"You know you're the only student who does this?"

"Well, those who don't are idiots." I carefully shut the jeep door without making too much noise. "I mean, look at all this space. There aren't even enough teachers here to fill it up."

He looks around, nodding. "I guess you're right."

"I am right."

We stand still, smiling at each other without saying a word. *We do that a lot.* Because he makes my chest feel funny, it's odd.

Regardless, I'll never get away with my unauthorized parking if he walks out of the lot with me. But I don't want him to go away either.

"Where's Riley?" I ask jokingly. I am curious to know what's going on between them. I mean, he's a Wek—I'm still trying to figure out what that means exactly—and isn't she human? How does a relationship work between them?

"I imagine she'll be here soon." He says that with a straight face.

"So…" I smile coyly. "What's really going on between you two? Is she not a human being? Is she like the devil? Because I would believe that, you know."

He chuckles a little bit. "No, she has no part with the evil, or me."

I frown. That was a weird answer. "Then why are you always with her like you're together?"

He shrugs. "Am I not supposed to talk to her if she wants to talk?"

I read his expression. He's seriously asking me that—like *seriously*.

"You know she likes you, right?" I ask.

"Yes, I do."

"No, she *likes* you. And it looks like you *like* her too, and that's what she tells everybody."

"I like all creation, Zill."

His expression is so sincere that it blows me away. I don't know what to say. All I can do is laugh. Riley thinks Derek is romantically interested in her when he's just a strange creature who only knows how to be nice to people. He's just giving her the attention she wants, which doesn't bother him at all because he doesn't get it.

"You know what she said once?" I stand there grinning at him.

"What?"

"That you said she was the best-looking girl in school, even better looking than me." I hold up my hands in my defense. "Believe me, I wasn't insulted. She's a very pretty girl and beauty's in the eye of the beholder, but—"

"According to the standards of humans, physically, she is the prettiest human girl in this institution. But you're not human, Zill."

"Yeah," I say sharply. "You mentioned that yesterday but refused to expound on it. Do you feel like elaborating this morning?"

The first bell buzzes. Then it's quiet again. I keep my eyes pinned to his face, waiting for an answer.

"You'll know soon enough. Things are already in motion."

I shake my head. "What does that mean, Derek?"

"Could I walk you to your class?" he asks, changing the subject.

"I wish. But if we walk out of here together, someone may see us and report that I'm parking over here."

"They already see us."

I follow his eyes across the woody mound of

land separating the student parking lot from the faculty side. Riley, Morgan, and two other girls are glaring at us past the spiny trees.

"Damn it," I curse under my breath. "After you."

TWELVE

I t sucks that my parking bliss is in jeopardy. He walks off, and I walk beside him, pretty sure I'll see Mrs. Lowenstein at some point during the day.

People eye us as we make our way down the hallway. I feel self-conscious because, for the first time, I can blame myself for their reaction. I purposely wore the jeans, a soft cashmere sweater, and black shiny boots. I can also blame myself for agreeing to walk the halls with Mr. Popularity. He's greeting just about everyone we pass, students, teachers and even the maintenance man in the gray jacket. I'm just the sour puss walking beside him, keeping my eyes forward until...

"Oh, Miss Decker, you're making friends!"

Mrs. Lowenstein sounds as if Derek and I walking together makes her the humble winner of what's behind door number three. She's standing in the doorway of the main office, peering at us.

"Good morning, Mrs. Lowenstein," Derek says, nice and cheery enough to cover the both of us. If anyone else said it like that, then it would've sounded creepy. He just sounds charming.

"Well, good morning, Mr. Firth," Mrs. Lowenstein replies, matching his enthusiasm. She cranes her neck to see me. Her eyes are expectant.

I lift a heavy hand and barely say, "Morning."

"Three o'clock in my office," she manages to sing through that tight-lipped smile.

"Of course," I call back after we pass her.

Derek touches my shoulder. "It'll be okay. She's just worried about you. She cares."

I look at him with a confused frown. Then I turn around to see Mrs. Lowenstein watching us with a proud smile. She clearly thinks that putting us together to serve punch the other night worked. I don't say it loud, but I guess he's right.

When we get to my first class, which happens to be homeroom, we stop in the middle of the doorway and face each other.

"Are you eating lunch today?" he asks.

Two girls entering the classroom hear him, and their eyes expand.

"No. I usually go home for lunch," I answer. I'm embarrassed because the entire class is looking at us, even the boys.

"How about you stay here today, and we can grab something together?" he persists.

Something about Derek Firth is extremely attractive. He can be whatever I need him to be. Not only for me, but for people like Riley Simms too. That's why she likes him so much. But he's a Wek. He's a beautiful Wek, charming, and someone who stirs up a feminine side in me that I thought never existed. Unlike Riley, I won't get sucked into the hole of what can probably never be.

"How about you do what you normally do and I do what I normally do?" I pat his chest.

He takes my hand and holds it against his chest. "Are you patronizing me?" He's wearing a tiny crooked smile.

"No," I say and then think about it. "Well, yes. But I mean it."

"Come on, Zill. We're friends now, aren't we?"

I sigh deeply. I never want to get too deeply involved in this school—just come and go, avoiding attachment to anyone, then return to civilization.

That was the plan. But just looking at him, wanting to know everything about him, I feel as if I've known him forever. And the crazy part is, I feel as if he'll never leave. "Okay, lunch," I say before I think better of my response. "Lunch then." I can't take it back now. I'm all in.

THIRTEEN

By the time lunch period begins, I'm ready to forget having lunch with Derek and head home. It's not that I've lost interest in him. It only takes four high school classes to make me want to free myself from this place. It's all so monotonous. Gosh, I hate high school.

And that's why I rush down the front steps of the building, abandoning my lunch plans and heading home. I keep my head lowered, eyes fixed on the ground, hoping and praying I don't run into Derek or Mrs. Lowenstein. When I reach the bottom of the steps, two bright white sneakers are right in front of me. As I look up, I see dark jeans, a black wool coat, and a face so handsome it should be illegal.

"Derek," I whisper.

He's grinning like he's read me from here to next year. "You sound disappointed."

"A little," I say, separating my index finger and thumb a tiny bit.

THE CAFETERIA IS full of students. It's snowing, so everyone's inside. The line to the counter is long, and I fold my arms across my chest, thumping my fingers impatiently as Derek holds conversations with any and everybody.

"So where are you guys sitting?" a red-faced, brown-haired kid asks.

I grimace. Sitting and listening to this guy talk was not in the plan. He and Derek have been chatting for seven minutes about the New England Patriots and Indianapolis Colts game and how some guy named Peyton Manning tried the no-huddle offense. Derek mostly reacted to everything the kid said, not offering much in return. He managed to make it seem as though they are equal participants in the discussion, though. It must be a gift.

"Hey, why don't you guys just have lunch here? I'm going to head out." I begin backing out of line.

Derek takes my shoulder. "Preston, if you don't mind, Zill and I have lot to talk about."

"Zill?" Preston sounds shocked. That I snap at anyone who tries to shorten my name is pretty much common gossip.

"Yes." Derek's tone remains charming, and so does his smile.

I think Preston, like everyone else, falls to the power of Derek's smile. "Um, sure. Maybe tomorrow, all three of us." Preston stares at me for reassurance.

I'm not charming because I'm not Derek. "Absolutely not," I say in my best mocking tone. When I give Derek a side-eyed glance, he's frowning at me. I decide to be nicer. "I'm not eating in here tomorrow, just today and never again."

"Oh. Okay," Preston says. He seems relieved by my explanation. "Well, see you guys later."

I shake my head after he leaves. "Can you stop?" I say under my breath to Derek.

"Stop what?"

"Stop having conversations with people. Let's eat and get this over with."

He gives me that perplexed look again, like what I'm asking doesn't make sense. But does he have to engage everyone? It's ridiculous and exhausting. But he does as I ask and remains quiet while keeping that confounded expression.

I get a salad in a cardboard bowl that's wrapped with plastic and a bottle of water.

"Is that all you're eating?" he asks.

I look at his tray. He has pizza, green beans, and some sort of syrupy fruit thing. "What, are you my nutritionist too?" Gosh, I didn't mean to sound so harsh.

"No," he says. He's not even insulted, which makes me feel worse.

"I'm sorry. I didn't mean to talk to you like that."

He steps in front of me to pay for my lunch. He just smiles at me before he tells the cashier thank you and then shines those bright, straight white teeth at her too.

"Follow me," he whispers in my ear.

To my delight, we head out the door. I catch a glimpse of Riley across the cafeteria. She's sitting at a table with her two-dimensional friends, and neither she nor they look happy as they watch us.

DEREK LEADS me down the steps and toward the front entrance of the school. There's an unmarked door right before we get to the gate. He opens the door to a small classroom with about six desks and chairs in it.

"It's the tutoring room," he says.

"You're also a tutor?" I watch him pull two desks together to face each other.

"Yeah, I help out."

I shake my head, but I'm smiling. "Of course you do."

He eyes me curiously. "Does that bother you?"

"No," I answer. Then I think about it. "Well, yeah, kind of. I mean, if that's what you do, then that's fine. But if you could just not do it while you're with me, that'd be great."

He gives me that confused look again.

"What?" I snap.

"You're not supposed to be this. What made you this way?"

"What way am I supposed to be? Happy? Because I'm not." I go stiff because I can't believe I just revealed that.

Derek doesn't say anything. I don't know what expression he's wearing because I'm staring at the wall.

"It's just…" I say. "The world is big, but I feel trapped in a tight space. That's all." After successfully willing myself not to cry, I look at him.

He's smiling understandingly. It's comforting. "Do you have any more questions for me?" he quietly asks.

"Um…" I inch back to look at him. There's no judgment in his expression, which causes me to give an inner sigh of relief. "I have questions."

"Shoot." He presses his back against the seat, getting comfortable in his chair.

"Okay, well, the other night, you said that the three guys were different from the other one. You know the one, who—"

"Yes, I know," he says. "Normally I can pick up on Selells' energy. I knew the fog rolled in, but we thought they were just passing through."

"Who are we?"

"Lux and…" He makes sure he can read every part of my face before he says, "Deanna."

I take a long time to blink. I actually see the black behind my eyelids for a little while. "Do you mean my mother?"

"Yes." He holds on to the last part of the word as if he wants to reveal more but can't.

I'm not shocked. Now her strange phone call makes sense. "So she knows about the Life Blood."

Again, he pauses. I think he's checking with himself to make sure he's able to answer that question. "Yes."

"All right, fine," I say to put him at ease. "So your being unable to pick up on the other three vampires, is that bad?"

"I don't know." He looks away. "They were different than the average Selell, and that's not good. Something's going on, but we'll figure it out."

"But what about the one that was hurt?"

"I think you had something to do with me being unable to get a read on him."

"Me?"

"This school has protection on it, and so does your house. He went undetected on your place of protection."

"But so did the other three."

"Yeah, but not because of you," he says.

I nod, trying to process all of this information. I don't understand how I could have kept Derek from sensing the vampire that was hurt. That reminds me of something else I wanted to ask him. "Who did that to his neck?"

"They were trying to drink him. Selells will die if they drink another Selell, which means those three creatures had to be another species of vampires."

"Wow," is all I can say because I have nothing to add to the facts.

He nods at my salad. "Do you eat meat?"

I think about it. I've never made a conscious decision not to eat meat. "No, I guess I don't."

"Interesting," he says.

"What's interesting about it?" He keeps his mouth shut tight. "Can't tell me?"

"Not at this moment."

I'm learning not to push him. Instead, I unwrap my salad and stab into the vegetables with the plastic fork. Then something strange happens. When I look up from my salad, Derek slides the backs of his fingers down my cheek. I'm immobilized by his touch, and I wonder what he's thinking.

"What? Why did you do that?" I ask, unfiltered.

"I don't know." He does look confused. "You're just a very beautiful creation."

"Oh." I stare into my salad. I can't believe I'm falling for a Wek. Although I don't know what a Wek is entirely, I know liking him in a romantic way wouldn't be that smart.

It's like we ran out of words. I have so many

questions to ask him, but I still feel his hand on my cheek although he's no longer touching me. I notice that he hasn't started eating yet.

"Don't like the pizza?" I ask between bites.

"I don't eat human food."

"But you ate the candy apple."

"It's not that I can't eat human food. I just don't. But the candy apples…" He nods. "They're good."

"Ha," I scoff. "We all have our vices, don't we?"

"What's yours?" he asks.

"A large, hot mochaccino at *Macchiato Espresso Bar* off Forty-Fourth and Lexington," I answer with a faraway look in my eyes. "And *Abraco* too. They make a great cappuccino." I sigh. "Gosh, I miss New York. You know, the convenience of it." When I look at him again, he's smiling. I smile back at him and say, "But now that I'm here in Moonridge, I'm with you. All it took was one bite into that candy apple, and now I'm addicted."

We both laugh as the bell rings. I ask Derek not to walk me to my next class. I don't think I can put on an indifferent face while he chats up every single person in the school. Once again, he looks at me as though he doesn't understand why that bothers me so much. Truth be told, I don't really understand.

When it happens, I don't feel like I'm being authentic.

"I mean, there are just some conversations I'd rather not have or listen to because I'm not interested," I try to explain.

"But it doesn't hurt to listen." He sounds too sensible.

I roll my eyes a little. "Well, it kind of does hurt me if I listen to someone blab on about nothing interesting. I get a headache."

"Really?" He has a serious expression.

"Really." Not really, but I go with it because although the headache is not literal, it is figurative.

He steps closer to me. Our faces are close. His breath smells faintly like cinnamon spice.

"Do I give you a headache?" he asks.

I lean away slightly, not repulsed, but definitely taken aback. "Are you flirting with me right now?"

"I don't know. Am I?" he says.

And the longer I look at him, the more I think he's asking me a serious question.

"Oh, Derek," I say, patting him on the shoulder as I chuckle and turn to my next, boring class. "Have a great rest of your day."

FOURTEEN

While in English Lit, all I can think about is Derek. Why did I lean away? Why did I laugh? I'm starting to think I should take him more seriously. I don't think he knows the difference between flirting and being kind. Poor Riley, she never stood a chance. But… I think I would've liked to kiss him. Just to see how he handles it.

"Any thoughts, Zillael?" Mr. Reynolds asks.

That's when I realize I've been daydreaming and staring out the window. "On what?" I'm slightly peeved by him putting me on the spot like this.

"Well, you would know if you were listening."

I glower at him for trying to patronize me. I've listened to his boring lectures every day, and he's acting as if all the other times I sat here pretending not to be bored out of my mind don't even count. Instinctively, I prepare the most sarcastic comment I can conjure. Then, and strangely enough, I ask myself what would Derek do?

When the answer comes to me, I sit up straight, look Mr. Reynolds in the eyes, and say, "Sorry, I'll pay closer attention."

The shock in the air is thick. I'm aware that everyone in the classroom expected a snarky remark from me, including Mr. Reynolds.

"Thank you." It sounds as though he's questioning whether I'm being authentic. "Thank you," he repeats more assuredly after a brief pause.

I almost shrink in my seat because I'm getting hit with stares. I make it a point to listen to every word Mr. Reynolds says about The Great Gatsby, which was this week's assigned reading. I had already read the book long before this week, and I have my thoughts on it. Hope he doesn't ask them. I don't want to talk about gluttony and privilege, and a guy who's such a nitwit he's too stupid to see that the woman he's pursuing has never been worth it.

FINALLY, it's the last class of the day. When I walk through the door, Mr. Lux is at the front of the room with his back to us, writing on the whiteboard. As I stand there watching him, Riley walks by and bumps me hard. The impact is like getting hit by a flea, but I'm still irritated.

"Oops, sorry," she says. Her snide smile tells me she's not sorry at all.

I'm debating whether or not to take her by the collar and hem her up against the wall in hopes it will scare her enough to figure out I'm someone she doesn't want to mess with.

"Zillael," Mr. Lux says as he whips around and dashes over to a chair in the front row on the opposite side of the classroom. He slams his hands on the tabletop. "Sit here."

Feeling hot under my black turtleneck, I move over to the seat.

Riley leaps in front of me. "So what's going on between you and Derek?"

"None of your business," I say past clenched teeth.

"How does it feel to screw around with another girl's boyfriend?"

"I don't know, never done that before," I snap.

"You're such a bitch," she bites back.

I try to picture what Derek would do in this case as well. I look deep into her face to really *see* her. There's vulnerability in her eyes. She's really young, probably the jewel of both her parents' eyes. With her light auburn hair and button nose, she should be a Christmas ornament. Mr. and Mrs. Simms would never believe their daughter's a bully. Another thing I see is that she really believes I'm unable to hurt her and thinks she can hurt me.

I know this is a dire situation because it's clear she won't stop taunting me until something severe happens. "Yeah, I guess so," I whisper hotly and step around her.

That's when she pushes me in the back. This time, I'm prepared. She shoved me hard, but I don't budge. My feet are planted, muscles contracted.

"Ouch," she screams and cradles the wrist of the hand she did the pushing with.

Morgan Slater and some girl whose name I think is Debbie rush over to see to her needs. I narrow my eyes at Mr. Lux as I pass him.

It wasn't my fault, I think, not sure if he hears me or not.

I know, I hear.

I stop in my tracks, shocked. I'm not crazy; he heard me, and I heard him, just like I've heard him before.

CHAPTER

FIFTEEN

Morgan accompanies Riley to the nurse's office, and class goes on as usual. Funny how fresh the air is without her. I didn't realize how much she taints my peace of mind.

At three o'clock on the dot, I knock on Mrs. Lowenstein's door, which has her name spelled out in black letters.

"Come in," she calls.

When I enter, she's wearing a genuine smile, and the smell of coffee slides up my nose. Mrs. Lowenstein takes a sip of coffee from a white cardboard cup.

"Moonridge has a Starbucks now." She raises her eyebrows at me with delight and motions toward another cup sitting on the desk. "Would you like a hot mochaccino?"

I grin from ear to ear, wondering if Derek mentioned my "vice" to her. If so, why would she supply it for me?

Our meeting is brief. Her condescending, smug smile is nonexistent. I learn that she hung new lime curtains in her living room last weekend but afterward realized they were ugly and took them down. She's thinking about taking a job in Cleveland, Ohio, but she doesn't want to leave Moonridge because she thinks it's enchanting. However, she's turning thirty-five in February, and she thinks it's time to recognize that she's actually divorced and it's time to start over.

I must admit, I'm stunned that she revealed that to me. As a matter of fact, I said absolutely nothing the entire time.

When she dismisses me, she says, "I'm sure I won't have to see you in here anymore. It looks like Mr. Firth has been an excellent influence on you."

I clamp my lips tightly to keep from exploding with laughter. That's when it occurs to me that Derek's influence over our crazy meeting went beyond the macchiato. I feel as though he's allowing me to be privy to the sorts of conversations he has with people, where they pour out their souls to him.

WHEN I REACH the parking lot, a tall figure is leaning casually against the driver's side of my jeep. As soon as he senses my presence, he turns and smirks. I can't help but stifle a laugh before making my way over to him.

"Do you have a headache?" he asks, still smirking.

I burst out into laughter. I can't believe he did that. It's the funniest thing that's happened to me since…well, ever! "No, I guess I don't. But that was too weird."

"Well, it wasn't a mochaccino from Macchiato, but hey, it's Starbucks."

"Yeah, and you convinced her to fetch me coffee? How did you do that?"

"I'm a Wek."

I grin at him, pondering. He's a Wek, and slowly, everything about him is becoming clearer, like pieces of a puzzle falling into place. "So, where do Weks go when everyone else heads home?"

He looks at me for a long moment. "You'll see where I'm from one day."

I nod, accepting his answer. "Do Weks sleep?"

"No, I don't sleep."

I study his face, trying to grasp how someone who looks so normal—flesh, bones, skin—can function without the need to sleep or eat. My thoughts drift back to earlier, after we had lunch, when he called me a beautiful creation. I wonder, can Weks even love?

"So you don't eat, don't sleep—what about the bathroom? Do you do that?" I ask, my curiosity getting the better of me. My own biology is strange enough in that regard.

"No, I never have to do that," he replies calmly.

"Oh." My brows furrow in surprise. Part of me hesitates, but then again, everyone else seems to share their secrets with him. Why not me? "I'm kind of limited in that department too. I mean, I can go, but barely. It's pretty rare."

"That would be logical," he says, as if it's the most natural thing in the world.

I flinch in surprise. "It is?"

"I told you, you're not human. Well, not fully. Your body can't absorb some human substances, and you will expel them in the human way."

I nod, again pondering what he just revealed. I haven't started my period either. The only reason I know I'm supposed to get one is because I've heard other girls talk about it. I'm supposed to bleed each month for five days. There are cramps, moodiness, and stomach bloating. I have none of that, and I'm a fully developed woman.

I'm seventeen years old, but I'm not built that way. The girls at my school look so much younger, so girlish. Even Riley Simms. I'm sure that's why I never take her seriously. She's like a kid who doesn't know any better. I'm like a freak of nature who doesn't belong with others who are my biological age.

After graduation, I don't know what I'll do. I'm not looking forward to college. I am looking forward to being in control of my life, which will involve moving far away from Moonridge.

Snow flurries sprinkle down, reminding me how cold it is. "I guess I should get home. Homework."

"Okay." There's hesitancy in his demeanor.

"What?" I ask.

"Nothing. I'll see you tomorrow?"

I swallow hard. I'm not sure what I want. This is so bizarre. I don't want him to go away. I want to do something like touch him or kiss him.

"Yes," I say and hurry up and get inside of my jeep. Once I'm inside, he taps on the window. I roll it down.

"Are you driving or walking tomorrow?"

I look down at my shoes and fitted jeans. "Definitely walking." I will never wear anything like what I have on ever again.

"I'll see you in the morning then," he says and walks off.

I watch him through my rearview mirror, wondering where he's going.

THE SELELL

SIXTEEN

When I arrive home and walk through the front door, I half expect to discover Deanna here. But nope, she's still away. I go into the kitchen to see if there's a message on the machine. There are two.

"I'm in Manhattan. I'll see you soon." It's Deanna.

I shake my head. At what point should I dig deep within myself and confess that I miss my mother? My eyes start to water, and since no one's around, I allow the tears to fall. And hell, I want to be in Manhattan too!

After swiping the tears from my cheeks, I check the next message. There's nothing but static. I delete the second message and save the first.

It's time to get comfy. I kick off the ankle boots, peel off my jeans, and then my sweater. I throw on the first pair of pajama bottoms I dig out of the drawer and an old, faded gray T-shirt. *Gosh, that's freeing.*

I bounce back into the kitchen to make a salad. After pouring myself a glass of water, I carry my dinner to the table to do my homework. The hours pass by, and by the time I finish, it's a little after ten p.m. Since I'm not a TV watcher, I go directly to bed.

In bed, I stare at the ceiling and abhor the next morning even before it starts. At some point, maybe an hour later, I close my eyes. Then my entire body turns warm, and though I'm unconscious, I'm sure something or someone is near me. My eyes pop open and blink to focus. I know I saw a white face looking over me, but now it, or *he*, is gone. I leap out of bed. Whoever it was moves fast, but I can too.

Our house surrounds an outside patio with a sliding, heat-activated glass roof that melts snow during the winter. I've learned to keep it closed all season long.

"Hey," I shout while racing down one hallway.

I hit the curve and zoom down the next hall. I see him standing in the patio, between the cushiony outdoor furniture circling the fire pit. His head hangs in surrender, arms limp at his sides. I stay cautious as I walk through the opened sliding glass door. I look up. The ceiling is open.

"Hey," I say much quieter. I'm looking at his back. It's extra dark tonight because the stars and moon are covered by snow clouds.

"Hey," he says back.

"Who are you?"

"My name is Vayle."

What a strange name. But so is Zillael. "I'm Zillael. Or do you know that already?"

"I know that." He turns to face me.

He's the guy from the other night, the Selell. I take a few steps closer. He doesn't look like a vampire, at least what I read about them. He *is* pale and anemic-looking, but his frame is healthy and strong. In everything I've read about them, they're extra beautiful. Now that we're standing face to face, I see that he *is* attractive, kind of sexy. But the Wek is more beautiful.

"What do you want?" I ask.

"I need help," Vayle mumbles. "This is the only place I can go."

"Why?" I remember what Derek told me about Vayle going undetected that night because of me.

"I don't know. But…"

"But what? Please tell me." I can't believe I'm begging.

"I haven't been thirsty since then."

"You mean that night?"

"Yeah."

He looks to be in his twenties. He's definitely not a high school-aged kid, which is good.

"Are you normally thirsty?" I ask.

"Ever since I became this…. Yes."

"Vampire?" I ask.

"Yes."

I take a few stops closer, not at all afraid of him. "When did this happen to you?"

"November eleventh, last year."

"Wow." I'm totally taken aback. "I thought vampires were, like, hundreds of years old." He seems so fragile, looking at me like he's lost, and I realize what I said was stupid and insensitive. "Sorry, I didn't mean it that way."

He shakes his head. "That's okay. I think I

might live to be a hundred years old, but this is the worst way to do it."

I nod in agreement, taking him in like he's a rare museum artifact. He looks so ordinary, so human. But so does Derek, and so do I.

I consider Derek's warning about Selells, but there's something about this Vayle guy. Maybe he's playing mind tricks on me, making me open up to him. Maybe that's why I ask, "Would you like to come inside?"

I watch him impatiently, so invested in his answer, during his long pause. I don't want him to turn me down. And I'm so relieved when he finally nods.

SEVENTEEN

I close the patio roof before leading him to the dining room, where we sit at the table facing each other. I would offer him something to drink, such as water, but according to folklore, vampires only drink blood. Inside, under the lights, he is quite remarkable looking. I wonder if he always looked like this, or if he changed after becoming a bloodthirsty creature.

"Where are you from?" I ask.

"Like where I was born?" he asks.

"Yeah."

"Illinois, but I used to go to the University of Maine."

"In Orono?"

"Yes—that's where it happened."

"Oh," I say, picturing what must be a town that looks a lot like this one. I would hate for something like that to happen to me while I'm here. Being turned into a vampire somewhere like New York City is way cooler. I want to tell him this, but I don't want to trivialize his experience either. Damn it. I've become much more thoughtful ever since Derek got into my head, and even, I think, my heart.

During our silence, I feel him staring at me, dissecting me, but I keep my eyes on the tabletop. I feel it too, our strange connection. I never thought I'd meet someone who seems as hapless as I am.

"Your parents are still in Illinois?" I ask.

"My whole family. Mom, dad, two sisters…"

I sit up a bit taller. "Do they know what happened to you?"

He gently shakes his head. "No."

I try to picture Vayle blending in with a family from Illinois. "You can't tell them," I say, more than ask. I really feel that he can't.

"Why should I?"

I think about that for a moment. I'm not the kind of person who reveals pieces of my soul to strangers, but I feel strangely compelled to now. "Well, I told my mother about being strong and fast, and how it scared me." I glance away, recalling how unbothered she had been. "But she just said she understood and told me not to be afraid of it."

He grunts. "That's because she knew."

"What?" I shake my head adamantly. "No. She didn't."

He peers at me, as if seeing through and around me.

"You're quick and can fight?" he says, flashing a lopsided grin, allowing my protestations to be. I sort of wish he would've negated me so that I could protest some more. Because…

I squeeze my eyes tight, not want to think about it.

"You okay?" he asks.

"I'm fine," I say, and conjure an odd and uncomfortable smile to prove it.

The air stands still as Vayle nods. Why do I feel so connected to him?

"Well.. What you were saying about my parents. I can't see them because I have no soul. No heart-beat. I am dead, and I crave blood. Only, I can't drink it from a human unless they offer me their blood. And they do offer it, they're as good as dead. Because I'm so fucking parched that I'll drink them dry. At least, that's what I heard."

I'm gripped by all he revealed as he searches my

eyes. "You mean you don't know? You're just guessing at this?"

I've been picking up bits and pieces. You know, because if I do—just try it, drinking someone dry without their permission—I could die. I've seen it happen. But…" He shakes his head. "But?" I ask. "I don't know. I think it's true. It has to be. My questioning is just hope. Because I've been so damn thirsty until…" His gaze sinks deeper into mine. "You."

We're staring at each other, and all I want to do is reach out and touch his face. This is a strange desire. What in the world is happening to me?

"It's called Parched?" I ask, past the tension in my throat.

"Yeah, my throat's been dry and hot. It always felt like it was going to crack open."

"And you don't feel it now, like right this very second." He shakes his head as his eyes water. "No." I shake my head, like I need to wake myself out of this... Not a nightmare because I've never felt so close to someone, even though he's a stronger, like I do to this Vayle person.

Then I remember something Derke told me, because even picturing something bad happening to this vampire sitting at my table makes my chest ache.

"Can I ask you something?" I look into his face, trying to assess if he's stable enough to answer my question. It's apparent he's still shocked and a little depressed by his predicament. The way he stares into my eyes lets me know I can ask. "I was told that those guys were trying to drink you. Is that true?"

His entire face frowns. "Yes, they were. I don't know how I got away. They were quicker and stronger than I was, but I managed to fight them off until I got to the school. Once I got there, it was like I got faster and stronger. But I'd already evaded them a couple of times, so…" He stares off down the hallway to the living room. "You ever watch those shows on Animal Planet where the gazelle is trying to get away from a pack of lions?"

I nod. I actually watch those programs all the time, whenever I decide to turn on the TV.

"I was the gazelle. They kept biting at me. And each time they struck me, I got weaker."

"Crazy," I whisper. I want to hug him or something, make all the bad memories go away. I want to reverse the unfortunate state he's found himself in, but I know I can't. "So what are you going to do now?"

"I don't know."

We fall silent again.

"But I'm sleepy now," he says. "I haven't been able to sleep since before I became this."

"Are you unable to sleep?"

"I've been too parched."

I look over my shoulder. We have a lot of empty bedrooms, all fully furnished by Rose, Deanna's interior designer from Hartford, Connecticut.

"You can sleep here tonight," I say.

"Can I stay with you?"

"You mean sleep with me?"

"Please." He sounds like he's begging.

I'm confused and don't know how to answer that. Sleep with me in my bed? Derek and Mr. Lux wouldn't like that. Heck, they wouldn't like the fact that he's actually at my table, alone with me. Supposedly I have the "Life Blood." I think Vayle is too new to the world of vampires to understand what that means. But if my touch makes him feel better, I want to help him.

"Sure," I say. "Why not?" I say, even though there are several reasons I shouldn't.

EIGHTEEN

y feet are heavy as I lead Vayle down the dark halls. What am I doing? Have I lost my mind? I'm actually about to go lie down in bed with a boy. A cute one at that. He's so fragile though. How can I be worried about the rule that *boys sleep separate from girls*? When we get to my room, I climb under the blankets, and he stands in the doorway watching me. I think he feels a little hesitant too.

I pat the empty space beside me. "Come on. Let's get this over with." I muster up an encouraging grin.

He moves so fast that I can hardly see it. He slides into bed beside me. We both lie on our backs, but he takes my hand. So we're holding hands and the sides of our bodies are touching. I feel genuinely *warm*. Warmth is filling me up, and it's strange as heck. I'm a little squeamish about it.

He asks, "Do you feel that?"

"I do," I quickly reply, glad it isn't in my head.

"So I'm a vampire, but what are you?" he asks.

"I have no idea, but I heard I'm something." I turn on my side to face him, and he turns to face me too. We grab hands again. "I guess we're both new to this."

He closes his eyes. "I guess so."

I watch as he drifts off to sleep, still holding my hand. A loud buzzing sound fills the air. I flick my eyes open to see that Vayle and I are no longer facing each other. He's cradling me tightly, but I'm able to wiggle free enough to fumble off the alarm.

What's strange is he doesn't even budge. He's, like, truly dead to the world. I mean, really *dead*. Today's a school day, and I think I have an excuse to stay home. Then I remember Derek is supposed to come over. I can't let him see Vayle here.

I get up and dig my cell phone out of a shoe-box. Deanna bought it for me two Christmases ago, and I keep it in the bottom of my closet. The battery needs to be charged of course, so I plug it in. I have Deanna's cell number programed in it. I only use the cell phone to call her, which I rarely do because *she's* always calling *me*. I need to make sure she won't show up today. Once I get it all plugged in, I pull her number on the contact list and push the button to call her. I hear two buzzes before she picks up.

"Z-cup, is everything okay?" she says, alarmed. She probably figured it must be serious if I'm calling.

"Yeah, I'm fine, Mom. I just want to know when you're coming home."

"Soon, honey. Is there fog this morning?"

"No, but…" I stop myself. If Vayle wasn't here, I probably would've tried to shame her into showing up like she'd promised. On one hand, I want her here, like a mother should be. On the other hand, I'm harboring who I'm sure will be an unwelcome guest. "When will you be here? I need to know when."

"Look, I got pulled into this merger. It's going to take some time, but you're safe. That's all that matters."

I shake my head and shut my mouth tight. I'm angry with her. "Whatever." I want to hang up, but I'll never disrespect her like that.

"Are you upset? Don't be upset."

I roll my eyes. I want to say I'm not, but I am, so I don't say anything. "Just when will you be home?"

"Next week, maybe. But I'll call you every day."

"Okay," I barely say. I want to cry, like break out into the cry of a heartbroken eight-year-old who misses her mommy. She's been traveling all of my life, and I'm tired of it.

When she hangs up, I drag myself to the bathroom to wash my face. Maybe I should've begged her to at least be home by tomorrow. That would still give me time to deal with Vayle. I'm sure he has to eventually go off to where vampires live. When the ice-cold water finally warms up, I splash it over my face. That's when I really start to cry. More than missing her, I'm just so lonely.

"Are you okay?" I hear behind me, and I jump and whip around. There's Vayle.

"Yeah," I say, sniffing.

He slides a finger down my cheek. "But you're crying."

"Oh." I'm lost for words, wondering how he could distinguish the water from the tears. Plus, I'm embarrassed. I'm a little too old to be crying for my mommy. I take one last deep inale to clog up the water works. "So what do vampires do all day?" I put on a genuine smile.

He still shows some residual distress. "Avoid the sun."

I point upward. The bathroom has the same glass roof that's over the patio. "But you're standing in the sun now."

We both look up. Though it's not directly above, sunlight is flooding in because the clouds are breaking up.

He holds out his bare arms and studies them. "I'm not burning," he whispers with wonderment.

"Have you burned before?" I ask. Although I know nothing about his experiences being a vampire, I find myself being pulled in to this miracle.

"Yeah, a lot."

We stare at each other. He studies his arms again as if he's waiting for them to burn at any moment.

"I don't think it's going to happen," I say.

He smiles at me. It's the first time I've seen him do that.

"I don't think so either," he says, still beaming.

"So now what are you going to do with your day?"

Wearing a crooked smile, he lifts his eyebrows at me. "I don't know, but the sky's the limit, isn't it?"

I almost feel jealous. I wish the sky were the limit for my day as well. I'm ill-equipped to go running off in a vampire's world. Then I remember Derek will be here soon.

"I have to get ready for school," I say.

"Can I go with you?"

"No way!"

He narrows his eyes at me, but he's grinning too. "Okay." He walks out of the bathroom with his hands behind his back like a little boy who's decided to be naughty.

NINETEEN

When I step outside, the cold engulfs me. Our entire property is covered with snow. When I get home, I'll have to shovel the driveway and walkway. That only takes me a couple of minutes. I glance over my shoulder at the door. I want to go back inside and forget about school. I almost convince myself to do just that when I look down where the sidewalk is covered in snow and see Derek waving at me. The next thing I know, he's standing right in front of me. That's how swift he moves. Everybody I'm meeting lately can move fast—even me.

"Hey," he says, grinning, eyes shining as if he's overjoyed to see me.

"I could've come down there," I say.

I'm working hard to be my usual self; I don't want him to suspect that I have a guest. The last time they met, Derek wanted to kill Vayle. Mr. Lux would've if he hadn't gotten away. I think their only mission is to keep Selells away from me. But what if Vayle isn't that kind of Selell? The type that needs to stay away from me? I'm on the verge of explaining that Derek, but something tells me not to.

"Everything okay?" he asks.

"Yes." I try to relax a bit more.

He narrows an eye. "Are you sure?"

"Yeah, I'm just, um…" I try to come up with a valid excuse. "I called my mother this morning, and she's not coming home yet, so…"

"Oh, I see. And you're upset by it?" he asks with that unemotional look of his.

I blurt out a laugh. That was the strangest response ever to me admitting some inner struggle with being left alone for a longer period of time. It's like he doesn't understand the idea of missing a parent. And frankly, I find it kind of refreshing.

"Anyway," I pat him on the shoulder to hurry him along. His nonchalant response has made me feel better already. "Let's go, Wek, before we're late." I smile at him, and he smiles back.

WE WALK UP the road quickly but not as fast as he moved to my door. I live pretty far from school and am definitely the only person who walks from there. Only a handful of students live in Main Valley, a vast stretch of land where a bunch of people from big cities decided to build rural palaces and live in them during the summer and some weekends in the spring. All of their kids attend boarding school or are lucky enough to remain in the city and go to school. I sulk about that every morning while taking this walk but not today.

Derek's quiet too. I take a quick glance at him. As usual, he smells really good and looks good too. We're such a paradox. I'm back to wearing what Deanna has termed "hobo gear." He's wearing a fresh pair of blue jeans, a soft, cream-colored, preppy high V-neck sweater, a brown leather coat, and brown loafers. Those strange dark emerald eyes are bright this morning, and his beautiful face is radiant.

"What?" he asks, grinning at me.

That's when I realize I too am grinning from ear to ear. "Nothing." Then I decide it doesn't hurt to ask him what I'm thinking. "Well, yeah something."

"What?" His interest is definitely piqued.

"Do you look and smell like this because you're a Wek?"

"Like what?"

I shrug because I feel self-conscious. I feel as though I'm revealing what I want to keep secret. "Attractive, I guess." I look down at the snow.

"You think I'm attractive?"

I peek at him, and his sly grin makes it clear that he knows how uncomfortable I am.

"No," I answer.

He just nods. "She thinks I'm good-looking and smell good."

I sigh hard. "Okay, yes, I do. So is it because you're a Wek?"

"Isn't attraction subjective?"

"What do you mean by subjective?"

"To some I may be attractive, but to others, I'm not. It's all about what the attracted finds attractive."

I blurt a cynical chuckle. "Was that a riddle?"

"Did you not understand it?"

"Yeah," I admit. "I understood it, but did you have to say it that way?"

His loud laugh fills the cold air around us. I smile at how genuine it sounded. I think he finds me amusing, which I do indeed find interesting. I've never thought of myself as an amusing person, just a cranky one. When he stops laughing, I stare at him without shame. I want to tell him about the vampire named Vayle who's hiding in my house. But I don't. I would never betray Vayle that way. He looks at me too. We're actually sharing a moment.

"How about we get candy apples for lunch today?" he asks.

"Now that's the perfect idea," I answer, still smiling.

A loud series of honks sound off, and we both look toward the road. A tiny red compact car with chains on the tires rolls past us. I take a closer look at the driver. Riley Simms glares at us with narrowed eyes.

"You know, you really have to—"I touch Derek's shoulder. I feel a rush of energy shoot through me, and I snatch my hand back.

He watches me with wide eyes, so I know he felt it too. What do these physical reactions mean? The vampire fills me with warmth, but the Wek makes my soul flutter.

"I have to what?" he says, breathing heavily.

I'm attempting to settle my rapid breaths too. "Talk to her."

"Okay," he says.

"Okay," I say.

TWENTY

W e walk the rest of the way in silence, both trying to figure out what just happened between us.

For the first time ever, homeroom goes by in a flash. During second period, I try to be attentive until something makes me glance over at the frosted Plexiglas at the top of the door. I see a boy staring at me.

"Vayle?" I whisper.

The kid in front of me, whose name I've never been able to remember, turns around to glance at me. My hand shoots up.

Mr. Carr stops explaining scarcity, which he just told us is one of the ten major principles of economics. "Yes, Zillael?" He always uses a strange emphasis when he says my name.

"Can I go to the restroom?"

He lifts his beaked nose. "Class, this is not kindergarten. If you have to go, then by all means, go." He continues with the lecture.

I take that as a yes. When he turns his back to write something on the whiteboard, I snatch up my book bag and dash out of the room. The entire class watches me leave. I'm clearly not planning on coming back. When I get out into the hall, Vayle stands there grinning at me.

"I knew you had the guts to cut out of there," he says.

I shush him. "What are you doing here?" I whisper.

Mr. Lux's classroom is just down the way, and Derek could appear at any moment. Standing in the open is not safe for him.

"Are we whispering?" He dips his face close to mine.

I take his arm and drag him along. I keep checking in front of me for Derek and behind me for Mr. Lux. I still don't feel safe when we're outside. I would use my speed to get us away from campus as fast as possible, but a few students are lingering on the sidewalks. They're always watching. *Small towns*.

We make it to the field that separates the student and faculty parking lots. I survey the area to make sure Derek or Mr. Lux haven't spotted us. The school buildings look peaceful, and there's not a soul in either parking lot.

"I was thinking," Vayle says.

I stop surveying our surroundings and put my eyes on him. "What?" I sound impatient.

"You want to come with me?"

"What? Where?"

"Back to Orono. I want to check something out in the day time."

At first, my expression drops because I'm wondering if he's lost his mind. "I can't just pick up and go to Orono." Then my expression widens because I haven't even convinced myself.

He grins at me. "But you want to go, don't you?"

I chew nervously on the side of my mouth. Then I narrow my eyes at him.

TWENTY-ONE

"You want to walk?" I ask, surprised by what he just said.

We've started up Main Street. I intended to drive us to Orono in my jeep.

"No," he says.

I stop, confused. "You want to take the bus?"

His grin grows wider. "No. Zill. We're going to ride the wind."

I stare up the road, thinking about the wind. There is no wind. And then, Vayle takes off.

"Keep up," he shouts.

I have no time to hesitate, so I take off after him. In a flash, we've made it to the end of Main Street and are shooting through the woods.

"Told you," he shouts.

What's surprising is how keen my senses are. I'm not going so fast that I don't see a tree in my path. I have to cut right a little to avoid it. We're following the natural Indian trails that cut through the forest. I smell the wet leaves, soggy ground, and clean snow. The surrounding ice is setting the temperature. My teeth chatter as my skin freezes, and Vayle glances back at me.

"Are you cold?" he asks.

"A little," I say past my tight jaw.

He reaches back. "Take my hand."

As soon as I grab hold, my entire body warms up.

"Better?"

My jaw loosens finally, and I'm able to say, "Yeah."

He gives me that grin again. What's strange is we're moving really quickly, but we don't have to shout to hear each other. I'm not winded either. I don't feel as though I'm expending much energy at all.

We pass some beautiful areas, including a number of shallow, snow-covered gullies surrounded by tall evergreens. Natural lakes cut through the forests. Every now and then, we'll pass a cute cabin or a deer in the snow. It's funny because the deer appear confused once they sense us. At first, they stutter-step to run for their lives, but then they stop and lower their heads docilely. It's quite humorous.

WE ARRIVE in Orono in minutes, not hours. The town doesn't look much different from Moonridge. We pass a red-brick building with a white steeple roof, and then another one, and then another one. We move until we end up in a parking lot facing a big blue "M."

"Maybe you are a vampire," he says to me with a wink.

I'm still shocked we actually ended up here the way we did. "Well, I'm something. I just wish someone would tell me what that is."

"Your date can't tell you?"

"My date?" I'm trying figure out what in the world he's talking about.

"Wasn't he there that night? He wanted to kill me, didn't he?" Vayle asks.

"Oh, Derek."

"Is that his name?"

I look around. I don't want to talk about Derek.

I just remembered we're supposed to meet for lunch, and I totally blew him off. Sitting on the bench in town square sharing a candy apple with him again would've been nice. That's probably why I accepted Vayle's invitation to skip the rest of the school day. I'm not sure it's wise to get involved with a Wek, someone who's supposed to be my guardian. Especially when I feel this natural pull to a vampire, or a Selell, or whatever. He mostly looks human to me.

"Why are we here anyway?" I ask with a bite.

Vayle reads my body language. I'm also questioning whether it was wise to make this trip with him. "Okay, we won't talk about *Derek* again," he says.

"Agreed," I quickly say. "Now, why are we here?"

"I think I want to see what happens when the presumed dead comes back to life."

I frown, confused.

"Come on, I'll show you."

TWENTY-TWO

This is a full-on school day, and the campus is alive. Students are hoofing it to their next class, and I'm checking out what the college looks like. It's quaint with lots of block buildings stacked close together, giving the place a toasty feel. It's funny because, simply put, the campus looks like a photograph of every college I've seen in America. There's a subliminal message to the design that says the act of retaining knowledge is a historical feat.

We end up in a wide, grassy area lined by trees. About three inches of snow frost the grass, but students still manage to track across it. Vayle is still holding my hand for warmth. We look like a couple, and a very interesting one at that. Each person we pass takes a second glance at us. This isn't high school, though. They don't ogle, just a couple of quick looks, and that's it.

"Do you have any friends here?" I ask as Vayle pulls me behind a tree. We stop and gaze out over the quad.

"Had friends here? Yeah, I did."

"Do you think anybody recognizes you?" Finally, the right time has come for me to find out something about him. I'm eager to hear his answer.

"They won't recognize me."

"Why?"

"Come on, Zillael, you already figured out."

"Because you don't look the same?"

He shakes his head while pressing his lips together. After a long silence, he says, "You can tell I'm the same person if you look hard enough, but there are differences."

"Like what?" I almost feel like I'm pressing him too hard, but I really want to know the answer.

"My eyes are black. They used to be blue. I'm whiter than I used to be. I'm taller and thicker too. I used to be pretty scrawny."

"Gosh, I wonder what's up with the changes." I didn't mean to say that out loud.

"Me too," he whispers. Then he squeezes my hand tighter. "There she is."

Too many people are crossing the quad for me to zero in on who he's referring to.

"Who?" I ask, eager for him to point her out.

"The girl in the gray trench coat. Black cap, long blonde hair," he says.

I search for a female figure wearing that attire, but I can't pick her out. It frustrates me.

"She just stopped walking," he says.

Then I see her. She digs into her book bag and takes out a little cell phone. She puts the device to her ear and talks into it.

"Is that your girlfriend?"

"Used to be."

"Wow," is all I can say. "Is this the first time you've seen her since you were——"

"No."

I turn to study him. "So you've been here since?"

"Many times, but at night while she's asleep."

"So you just, what? Watch her?" I ask.

"Yeah, that's it."

"That's kind of creepy."

He doesn't respond. I think he knows that's true.

He beams in on her. His eyes reflect his loss and heartache. "She's talking to Danny."

"You can hear her?" I'm stunned.

"Yeah."

"Sounds like you know Danny."

"Used to be a friend of mine. He moved in on her about a week after I went missing."

"Gosh, such a cliché."

He chuckles. "Yeah."

As the students trudge across the mall, they seem so oblivious. An actual vampire and a strange girl who can walk seventy-nine miles in twenty minutes or less are staring at them. They're all cold, but two groups of boys are tossing a football back and forth. A couple students have brushed snow off of a bench, laid something across the seat, and sat down, huddling to generate heat. Students face each other with packs on their backs or slung over their shoulders, smoking or sipping coffee, chatting away.

"You should go talk to her," I whisper after a long moment of silence.

"Should I?" He's apprehensive. He gives me a quick glance.

"You should," I say. "I mean, what do you have to lose?"

"I could scare her," he suggests.

"You can also put her at ease."

"Maybe…"

"Just go before it's too late."

We look at each other; the questioning is still in his eyes. Then he nods and starts off across the snow. His posture is straight, and his physique is superior. I'm admiring the way he moves, and a grave feeling hits me. What if after they speak, I never see him again? The pinch of loss I feel is crazy for sure. I mean, his absence will make my life much easier.

He stands in front of her. She's frozen in place with the phone pressed to her ear. He says something to her. Without thinking, her hand drops to her side and the phone falls into the snow. Vayle squats, picks it up, and hands it to her. She's still immobilized, too shocked to take it I guess, so he keeps it. Then he says something to her. After a long moment, she says something back.

"What are you doing here?" a person who just stepped up beside me asks.

I practically jump out of my skin and turn to see Derek.

CHAPTER

TWENTY-THREE

H is green eyes demand an answer.

I press my hand to my chest. Shock takes the wind out of me. "What are you doing here?" But then I think of a better question. "How did you find me?"

"I can find you anywhere. So what's going on?"

"Nothing," I say too quickly. I try to relax and not be so uptight.

"You're lying, Zill."

I don't say anything. He looks so upset by the fact that I *am* lying to him. He looks out over the mall. He sort of zeroes in on Vayle but then looks away.

"I just thought I'd come see what next year's

going to look like," I say, deciding to tell a boldface lie.

He stares straight ahead, watching the students. "We were supposed to hang out."

"I know." I look at him with repentance in my expression and then back out across the quad.

Vayle is walking with his girlfriend. They're side by side and glance at each other as they move forward.

"Who's that?" Derek asks, pointing at Vayle.

"Just a guy," I guess.

Derek scowls at him before he gazes up at the sky. I know he's considering the sun, questioning whether Vayle is a vampire or not. He's walking in the sunlight with no dense fog, and that probably throws Derek off.

"Is he someone you know?"

I try to sound as earnest as I possibly can. "No."

When I look over at Derek, he's staring at me. His face is unreadable, but the brightness that's usually there when he looks at me is gone.

"Do you still want to get that candy apple?" he finally asks.

"Sure." I'm working hard to relax, but I'm wondering where Vayle and his girlfriend have gone.

TWENTY-FOUR

I wish I knew what Derek was thinking. I follow him to a black truck in the parking lot with black tinted windows. He opens the passenger door for me, and I climb in. He hasn't looked at me or said anything more. As he navigates out of the parking lot, I hug myself tightly to get warm. He turns on the heater.

"Thanks," I say with a quick glance at him.

He keeps his eyes straight ahead. "You're welcome. Did you drive here?"

"Um, no."

"Then how did you get here?"

I hesitate. I've done enough lying for the day. "I walked."

"Eighty miles?"

"Yeah."

"By yourself?"

I nod timidly.

"You're lying." He sounds so disappointed. "You never have to lie to me, Zill. As your guardian, I encourage you not to."

I turn to look at him, and my heart is tight. "Are you mad at me?" I sound so pathetic, so fragile. I've actually shown vulnerability a lot lately, and I don't think well of it.

"No, I'm not."

I stare at his beautiful profile. I guess he has the right to be disappointed that I lied to him. All I remember is begging him not to kill Vayle. If Vayle hadn't found the strength to get away, Derek and Mr. Lux would've killed him.

I know Derek thinks he does what he does for my good, but killing Vayle would not be for my good. It's bizarre, but I'm attached to him. Not in a romantic way, I don't think, although it did sting a little to see him with his girlfriend. I feel as though I've known him forever and a part of me lives within him.

Derek glances at me staring at him. "What are you thinking?"

I shake my head. "Nothing."

He mashes his lips together. It's obvious he knows I'm thinking *something*. But I'm not telling until I know I can trust him with these feelings I have for the Selell. So I let him remain quiet for the rest of the trip.

THE DRIVE TAKES about an hour and a half. It's amazing how Vayle and I only took about twenty minutes by foot. What sort of person or thing am I? I've tried to push this question out of my mind for days. Each time the question creeps back to the forefront of my thoughts, I get a little frightened and push it back, trying to banish it for good.

Derek parks in one of the slanted spots along Main Street, gets out, and opens my door for me. We move up the damp wooden planks with snow trapped in the creases. When we get inside of Jake's Candy Apples, Derek is his old cheery self, grinning and happy to see Jake. Jake flirts with me of course, and for the first time since he appeared by my side earlier, Derek actually smiles at me as he hands me my candy apple.

We sit on the bench like last time to eat our apples. *Dear goodness, they taste so good.*

"You ever had Molly's Apple Pie?" he asks me.

"No, never. No." I try to draw my answer out to make sure we keep talking.

"It's good."

"Is it?"

"It is."

I'm waiting for him to ask me to try it with him one day, but he doesn't. I think I'm pouting. I'm pretty sure I'm hurt.

Then he says, "We should go there for lunch tomorrow."

I smile. "Okay."

I'm hopeful that he still likes me the same. At this moment, if I had to choose between the Wek and the vampire, I'd definitely choose the Wek. I could actually fall in love with the Wek because although he isn't a human being, he's the perfect human being.

We finish our candy apples. He asks if I'm ready to go home.

I say, "Yes, but I'll walk."

He scowls. I can't take the freeze out any longer, so I simply turn and lope up the wooden planks, hoping that tomorrow he'll be in a better mood. I run fast enough for every driver passing by to watch me curiously. It's a five-mile, all-out sprint. Normally I'd care who sees me galloping like a world-class athlete, but this time, I don't.

TWENTY-FIVE

When I enter the house, I feel the need to look out the window. I pull the thick curtains and search the road. Just as I thought, the black truck creeps by. I crack a slight smile.

"You're home," a familiar voice says.

I think I'm dreaming as I whip around. "Mom!"

"Hi, Z-cup!"

I walk really fast to her, restraining myself from running, and we hug tightly.

"I thought you weren't going to be here for a couple of weeks?" I ask after we let go.

"Plans changed."

My mother is wearing a gray skirt suit with

stockings and heels. I'm way taller than she is, and she's fairer than I am. She's the direct opposite of me in every way. My hair is jet black; she's blond. My eyes are yellow; hers are sea blue. She's petite and thin. I'm curvy but slender.

"I looked in the refrigerator, and all I saw was salad. Is that all you're eating?" she asks.

"Kind of. I had a candy apple today."

"Have you gone to the grocery store?"

"Not recently."

She rolls her eyes and walks toward the kitchen. I follow as she says, "I went grocery shopping for you. I'm going to make dinner tonight."

"Like what?" She knows how finicky I am.

"Pea soup and olive-stuffed spinach rolls. No cheese."

"Okay," I say, beaming. That sounds really good. It's been a long time since I've eaten a complex meal.

"How was school today?" she asks, pulling the freshly bought items out of the refrigerator.

I shrug. "Fine, I guess."

She narrows her eyes but doesn't say anything further about school. "I heard you met a new friend?"

Now *I'm* narrowing my eyes at *her*. "Yeah, I did."

"We'll talk about it during dinner. But why don't you go get comfortable for now?" She sighs and looks down to inspect herself. "I'll get comfortable too. I can't cook in this."

The entire house always smells like home when Deanna returns. She cooks, lights caramel-scented candles, and has a thing about scrubbing bathrooms until a fresh pine scent lingers in the air. She's never still, always replacing a light bulb or dusting a bookcase or something like that. Her presence fills every nook and cranny of what was an empty place. Now I feel truly safe.

I jump into my pajamas and T-shirt and sit on the foot of my bed. I don't have any homework since I skipped school today before any could be assigned. I take a deep sigh and lie back on the bed, wondering what happened between Vayle and his girlfriend. My mind creates all sorts of endings to their story. Maybe she begged him to change her into a vampire, and because he loves her so much, he did it. They'll spend eternity together, and he won't need my warmth anymore. Maybe from the moment he scratched on the cafeteria door until he laid his eyes on his love in daylight, I was his destiny for that very ending.

I'm sort of happy about that. I slide up to the top of the bed and cuddle up with the pillow. I close my eyes and think about Derek. I find myself catching a breath.

I'm naked, and I see him sliding his hands up from my pelvis to my belly button until they circle my waist. He's lying next to me on this bed in this moment.

"Look at me," he whispers.

I open my eyes. Our lips are millimeters away from each other. I'm breathing heavily.

"We should kiss, don't you think?" he asks.

Though I'm choked by desire, I manage to whisper, "Yes, I do."

I'm waiting to learn what kissing Derek would feel like when I hear, "Zillael!"

My eyes pop open. I'm in my bedroom, fully dressed in pajamas. "Yes, Mom?"

"Dinner!"

I look at the clock on the nightstand. I've been lying here for about an hour and half. I didn't even realize I fell asleep. I slide off the bed and walk into the kitchen. Deanna is already seated at the dining room table, and there's a place setting for me.

"You look exhausted," she says as I drag in.

"I am." I flop into my chair.

"Did you go on a long walk today?"

Again, I eye her suspiciously. "This friend of mine that you asked about earlier. Do you know him? Derek the Wek?"

"Yes, I do," she answers.

I nod during the silence. I thought so. Now that I remember, Derek mentioned knowing her. "How long have you known him?" I ask, keeping my eyes on the perfectly stuffed spinach roll set in a thick white crème sauce.

"Since the day you were birthed."

I look up at her. I feel myself frowning. "Did you know his mother or something?"

"Derek doesn't have a mother. He told you he's a Wek, right?"

"Yeah," I say leadingly, insinuating that she should continue explaining.

"He was created to watch you."

My frown becomes more disturbed than confused. "Why?"

She stares deep into my face. I've seen that look before. Like when I was eight years old and begged her to take me on a business trip with her. It's the *you already know the answer to that* look.

"Because I'm special somehow," I say, sounding like that eight-year-old who answered, *because mommy has to work and I have to go to school.*

"At some level you've accepted that, which was why you were able to take that long walk today. Did you take it alone?"

A picture of Vayle flashes in my mind. "Yes, I was alone."

"Good for you." She faintly smiles at me.

I look away because the lie so easily flowed out of my mouth. It's horrible that I'm lying for a guy I may never see again, who also happens to be a Selell, or vampire, or whatever.

"You are made of three beings, and only one quarter of you is human," she says.

I think I just lost my appetite. I look down to study my hands resting on the tabletop. I have five fingers. I have arms too. I touch my cheek—there's a face. "I don't understand."

"It will be confusing for a little while longer. It's not my place to tell you everything, but you'll meet someone soon who can."

"Who?" I sound desperate for an answer.

"Just someone." She nods at my plate. "Eat. You still need to nourish your human side."

The only problem is my appetite hasn't

returned. I rarely have an appetite anyway. I usually force myself to eat because I'm supposed to.

She watches me dip my spoon into the pea soup and drink it. "Good." She smiles. "You want to know if I'm really your mother, don't you?"

I swirl my spoon in the bowl of thick green liquid. The truth is I don't know. I've heard about kids who find out their parents aren't biologically theirs. I always imagined how horrible that would feel. To know all about the birthing process, how the mother toils in pain, creating a bond in itself, only to learn that's not how they came to be in the life of the person who raised them. The truth is, deep down, and I mean way deep down inside, I suspect I too had a story like that.

Deanna and I look too different. She still hasn't been able to produce one photo of my father. I figured she was one of those independent women who decided to pick her child out of a test tube. I even once toyed with the idea of her being a CIA agent, and I was created to one day fight the enemies of our country. Like that movie *Salt*, or something like that. Maybe that's why I can do what I can do.

I set my glossy eyes on her face and whisper, "You'll always be my mother."

Her expression remains wide and sort of confused. "I love you as a person loves a daughter as well."

Right there, my non-question has been answered. I am not biologically hers.

The human side of me is hungry again, so I take a few more sips of soup. "Can I ask you something else?"

"You can ask me anything, and if I can answer it, I will."

"Why did you come back early? You were supposed to return a few days ago because of the fog, but that went away. Why are you here now, today?"

"Because it's gotten infinitely more dangerous for you."

"How?"

"They're looking for you," she says.

"They?"

"Derek told you about the Life Blood, did he not?"

"Yes, but I thought he came up with that story after sniffing glue or something," I say with a weak grin.

"But knowing him now, do you believe him?" She's serious. Typically, she would detect my sarcasm, roll her eyes, and then all would be normal in the Decker household. This time, she didn't play along.

I swallow the lump in my throat. "I guess so. Although it makes no sense to me."

"It will."

"Okay, but when? Because you guys are saying a lot but not telling me anything." I'm a bit peeved, and I sound like it.

"I know, Z-cup." Her eyes caress me like they normally do when she aims to comfort me. "You'll know more soon enough."

"Okay, but did Derek tell you about what happened? How I fought those guys off and they were like Selells, which are actual vampires?"

"Yes, I know about them."

"Remember what I did to those girls?"

We look at each other. I suspect that's why she moved us here and forced me to attend the local high school while she went globetrotting. The way she looks at me provides the answer.

"Well, I actually killed one before Derek showed up and killed the other two. I think I broke his neck."

"You being able to do this, does it bother you?" she asks.

I think really hard. On one hand, they were trying to suck the blood out of Vayle, and then they wanted to kill me too. But if I dig deep down, there's only one true answer. "Yes, it bothers me that I killed him. But more than that, it bothers me that Derek killed the other two and that Mr. Lux used his sword to burn their bodies. Do you know Mr. Lux too?"

"Yes, I do know Lux. That was the right answer." She says the first part quickly but holds on to the second sentence a little longer.

"You mean feeling bad about the vampires being killed?"

"Yes. You've been created to preserve life, not take it."

I shake my head. "That doesn't make sense."

"I know it doesn't. Those guys chose to die because they chose to fight. I know that for someone like you, that's still not a good reason, but it was either you or them, wasn't it?"

"Yes," I quietly say.

"You're going to be faced with that same decision in the future, and you can't hesitate. Never hesitate." She leans into me. "Understand?"

I swallow the lump in my throat and bob my head.

"But… tonight, we're going to enjoy dinner together," she says with an air of lightness. She smiles broadly. "Come on, try it."

I realize I'm frowning, but I force myself to smile.

"Keep it going," she says, still smiling hard.

Finally we both laugh. This is why I love her so much. She always has a way of showing up and making the brief time we spend together worth the wait.

"Can I ask you something else?" I say once we simmer down.

"Go for it."

"Well…" Gosh I feel embarrassed. "Well…" I try again.

"Well…" She's leading me on.

"Weks," I say.

"What about Weks?"

"Can they like people? Like me?"

"Are you asking if Derek could like you?"

I study my plate. If I could blush, which I can't, my face would be blood red. "Yeah."

I'm prepared to hear no.

"Maybe," she says as the sides of her mouth turn down. "Have you asked him?"

"No," I answer too fast. "I mean, no," I say with much more control.

"You should."

"I should?"

"It wouldn't hurt."

"It wouldn't?"

She grins at me, detecting the double meaning in my question. "You've always been a clever one, but I won't provide you with the answer you want to hear. You have to be willing to hear the worst or the best and move forward with that answer."

I understand. She's right, and I tell her so.

"I know," she says with a wink.

I chuckle. "You know, Mom, you're like my own personal Yoda."

"Great! But what's a Yoda?" The look on her face tells me she's serious.

"Wow. You've never seen *The Empire Strikes Back*?"

"No, I can't say I have."

Sometimes she makes me wonder... Has she ever lived a normal life and experienced normal things? Even I saw *The Empire Strikes Back*, and that's saying a whole lot.

"Well, that's your homework for tonight, Mom. Go learn who Yoda is. You never know, not knowing this piece of American film history could make you lose out on a big business deal. The next tycoon you run into may be a *Star Wars* geek."

She throws her head back and laughs. "But I thought you said *The Empire Strikes Back*?"

My face drops. "Forget it." I shake my head. "You'll just lose out on that deal." We both laugh.

TWENTY-SIX

I decide to hit the pillow earlier than usual. That walk must've taken a lot out of me. Earlier, it sounded like Deanna connected the exercise with me looking exhausted. I forgot to ask her why. I finally feel like I can rest because she's home.

I strip off my pajamas and hop into the shower. I let the steam the running water generates engulf me as I massage shampoo through my mounds of hair, which will dry in minutes after I step out of the shower. That's another crazy fact about myself.

I can't sleep in my pajamas when Deanna is home because she cuts the heater up about five degrees. Normally, I'll end up pulling my clothes off during the night, so I just climb into bed wearing my bra and panties. As I lay in bed with the lights out, I dread tomorrow. Having to go to school hasn't changed, and since I skipped out on almost all of my classes today, Mrs. Lowenstein will be stalking me.

"Great," I mutter and turn on my side. Not even dread can keep me awake tonight.

At some time during in the night, I kick the covers off and flip over to lie on my other side. Out of nowhere, I feel a body push up against my backside.

I gasp, but before I can jump out of bed, Vayle whispers, "It's just me."

I ease up off the bed and tip toe across the floor to gently shut the door. I turn to face him. "You're back."

His mouth is wide open, and he looks mesmerized by something. I look down at myself.

"Oh my gosh," I say a little too loud and race across the floor while trying to cover my body with my arms.

"No, by all means, be free," he whispers, grinning with shining eyes.

I look around for my pajamas, but then I remember stuffing my last clean pair in the hamper, which is in the laundry room. So I dive back in bed and pull the covers around me. He's trying so hard not to laugh, and soon so am I. I looked ridiculous trying to hide myself. No one has ever seen me this close to being naked, not even Deanna.

"Listen," he whispers and looks at my door. I'm sure he knows I'm not alone. "You look hot, but I have bigger problems than wanting to bang you, at least right now."

"Wow, now that you put it like that…"

He's lying beside me, looking up at the ceiling, then he flips on his side. "But can we… you know?"

I sigh hard and pull the blanket off of me. In a really fast movement, he's behind me, pulling me into him. Even with the heater blowing out hot air, I feel warm and comfortable in his grasp. It's like our skin contact not only soothes the cold but the heat too.

My eyes are getting heavy again, but I manage to ask, "So how did it go with your girlfriend?"

After a long pause, he says, "She's scared of me."

"But does she believe you?"

He takes another long pause. "Yes."

"Will you ever see her again?"

"Not like this."

"Not like what?" I flip around to face him.

"No," he rephrases. "I'll never see her again because this will never change. Have you ever heard of a cure for being a vampire?"

I swallow hard, saddened by his predicament. "I haven't."

I think his eyes are tearing up. It seems private, so I flip back around to face the opposite direction. After a moment, he pulls me in closer. This time I feel different about it because his hands are sliding up and down my arm. He's throbbing in other places.

"You're soft," he whispers.

I don't know what's happening inside me. "That's the first time I ever heard that." I want to forget how his hard body, pressing against my back-side, tickles my insides.

"I bet you've never been kissed." He puts his lips on my bare shoulder and kisses it.

I swallow hard. *Tell him to stop.* "Why do you think that?"

He chuckles quietly. "It's true, isn't it?"

I don't respond because it is true. I've seen couples with their mouths pressed together at school. I've heard it happens a lot on television and in movies, but I barely turn on the TV and never head to my local theater and if I watch a movie, it's on DVD. I've heard of kissing being called *suck face* once, and that's exactly what it looks like: an unsanitary act of two people sucking off the other's face.

My stance against kissing has changed recently. If Derek put his lips on mine after we had lunch together, I wouldn't have resisted. I sort of wish he had done it. When Vayle asks, "Can I be your first kiss?" my mind ventures back to that very moment.

I turn to face my bed partner again and am taken aback by the lust in his eyes.

"This is all of a sudden, don't you think?" I whisper.

"Not for me. I can't stop thinking about how it will be to be with you."

"But your girlfriend?"

"I know," he says. There's that pain again. "I can't control what I feel for you. I want you all the time. I think I'm even jealous of that runt who walked you to school yesterday."

"I thought we weren't going to talk about him."

"Do you like him?" he asks.

I shrug.

"That's not an answer."

"I don't know." I cast my eyes down.

"You do," he concludes.

"I said I didn't know."

"I can feel that you do."

I frown at him.

"You don't get how connected we are yet, do you? If that guy wasn't around, you probably would."

"Maybe," I say. I'm consumed by my desire for Derek. I absolutely, unequivocally love to share space with him. As a matter of fact, if I was lying next to Derek right now, I'm sure I would've said yes to that kiss right away. Not that I don't want to kiss Vayle, because I do. But my heart feels like I'd betray Derek by doing so.

"What is he anyway? I know he's something."

"He's a Wek."

"A wreck?"

I chuckle a little bit. I know he mispronounced it on purpose. "No, a Wek. No *r*."

"He likes you too."

"I don't know," I admit. "He seems to like everyone. I think it's his nature."

"Maybe that's what you're attracted to, his nature and not him."

"How are the two separate?"

"Kiss me, and you'll see."

I hesitate. He's obviously putting the moves on me, and I'm obviously falling for it. It would be nice to have some sort of clarity on how I feel about Derek. I love how Derek likes everyone and how everyone likes him. He genuinely cares to listen to stuff I'd have little or no patience with. He's gorgeous. He's chivalrous. And he can really kick butt.

"You're like the apple, you know?" I say with a coy grin.

"Forbidden fruit." He gives me that wicked smile as he presses a finger against his lips. "Here, Zillael. Put your mouth here, and I'll do all the rest."

I don't hesitate. The mission is to get it over with, to finally be kissed and prove to myself that what I feel for Derek isn't romantic but pragmatic.

Our lips touch, and the next thing I know, he's on top of me. We're kissing, actually sucking face. He's gentle with me, which surprises me because his desire is so strong; I can feel it consuming me. Every touch of the tongue and lips is sensual.

"You taste sweet," he whispers between kisses. "It's been a long time since I've tasted anything sweet."

We look into each other's eyes. I haven't completely let go although my body wants to. His hands skillfully caress my back, neck, even nipples.

His mouth slides down to them. A breath escapes me because of the way it feels. Then his fingers are beneath my panties and touching me. He's doing something to me. I find myself grabbing him as I cry out after a rush of pure pleasure builds up and explodes.

"Shush," he says gently.

I look at the door. I cried out loud enough for Deanna to hear me if she's still up.

"Are you still a virgin, Zillael?" he whispers while kissing my mouth. He still hasn't moved his hand.

"Yes." I can imagine how timid I look because these physical feelings have immobilized me. These sexual sensations are new to me. The image of Derek that was stuck in my head before the vampire started his exploration of my body is foggy now. I'm still confused about how far I want Vayle to go.

He kisses me even more fervently as he moves his hand out of my panties. "Damn, you're a virgin. Oh damn!" He pulls back.

"What?" I'm alarmed.

"What's this?" He rubs a finger around a single area on my upper back.

Without looking, I know what he's referring to. "Birthmark. Why?"

He sits up, reaches over his shoulder, and touches his back. "Look."

I twist around him to see a birthmark that looks exactly like mine in the same spot. It's a perfect half-moon shape. "Strange." I think this discovery has calmed our lust, or at least masked it.

He lies down on his back again, staring at the ceiling. As soon as I lie back down on my side, he cradles me.

"Are we done?" I ask.

"Yeah," he answers.

After thinking about it, recalling how we were just all over each other, I laugh. What's funny is he laughs too. Finally we simmer down.

"I still want you so damn bad," he says. "Your first time will be with me, but you'll be over the Wek by then."

I smirk. "You sound pretty sure of yourself."

He pulls me closer. "I can't wait." He lifts my hair to kiss the back of my neck.

I turn my head to face him and kiss his lips again. I love how he tastes, but I have to turn away. He's right. The haze has lifted from the picture of Derek, and I see him more clearly. When I fall asleep, Derek is with me. We're walking to school again; he's holding my hand. I ask if he forgives me for kissing Vayle.

"Of course," he sings.

"I think I wanted him in a sexual way, and really bad too. Is that okay?"

"Of course," Derek says again.

"Do you want me in the same way?"

He runs a finger across my lips and then lowers his to kiss me. But it's a soft, quick kiss.

"See," he says, sounding unaffected. "It means nothing to me."

I hear my mother yell my name and wake me up. Both Vayle and I are shocked to see her. Her blue eyes are glowing orange, and the pretty, soft features of her face have given way to hardness.

"Mom?" My pulse is racing.

"Selell?" Deanna growls, stabbing Vayle with her eyes.

TWENTY-SEVEN

I don't know why, but I spread my arms out in front of him, protecting him from her. "Mom, wait."

It's too late. She moves like a blur. When she's done, all the curtains are all pulled open. I never do that because I like it dark inside. It's not a sunny day, but the light from the rising sun flows in through the windows. I believe that was her attempt to kill Vayle. When he doesn't burn, her mouth and eyes are agape.

"Mom," I shout louder. "Please."

Finally she looks at me. "Get away from him now, Zillael."

"No. Calm down so I can explain."

She looks crazed. "What are you?"

Vayle glances at me. "Vampire, I think." He doesn't sound sure.

"You should've burned," she says.

"I know," he and I say at the same time.

"It's because of me, we think," I say. Her eyes turn blue again, and I sigh with relief.

"Move," she orders me.

I'm still lying beside Vayle, and I realize that his arms are wrapped around me as well. He doesn't budge until I say, "Okay." I separate from him, and when we're apart, she does that blur movement thing.

She's in his face, inhaling him. Vayle and I watch her, confused.

"You *are* a vampire," she confirms. "I don't understand why you didn't burn."

"So you were trying to kill him?" I sound horrified.

"Yes," she answers. "For your own good."

Out of nowhere, Mr. Lux appears in the doorway holding that sword of his. It looks as if he's ready to fight at any time. I'm absorbing a couple of things at once, but when Derek rushes up behind Mr. Lux and his eyes fall over my scantily clad body, covering myself up becomes my number one priority. I scramble for a blanket and pull it up over me.

I think it's only when I cover myself that Deanna notices I'm wearing a pair of white cotton bikini-cut panties and a white cotton full-coverage bra. What's odd is her eyes just sweep over me, and that's the total of her reaction. I would think a parent, especially a mother, would lose her mind. Deanna doesn't, and for the first time, it's crystal clear to me that she's truly not my mother.

"Look, Lux," she says, referring to the curtains being pulled and Vayle sitting beside me, untouched by the sunrays.

Mr. Lux looks from the windows to Vayle and disengages his sword. Derek hasn't taken his eyes off of me since he showed up, and I can't stop trying to figure out what his expression means. I've never felt so apologetic, although I'm not sure why. He doesn't look mad or hurt, just blank.

STRANGERS IN THE FOG

TWENTY-EIGHT

We're all in the living room, the area with the most windows, and all the curtains are pulled. I've been given time to put on jeans and a T-shirt, and I'm standing beside Vayle in the middle of the living room. He's still under scrutiny, and I dare not leave his side. Mr. Lux, or Lux without the mister, keeps his hand close to that deadly sword of his. I already told Deanna about our birthmarks.

She's behind Vayle, lifting his shirt to study the mark on his back. "Derek, come see this."

Derek, who still hasn't said anything, hesitates before walking over.

"Look," Deanna says and then lifts my shirt to show him that I have the same mark.

When Derek touches me in that spot, I catch a breath. Although Deanna is holding my shirt up, he takes the hem and gently lowers it.

"It's the sign of the sun," he concludes.

"Elaborate." It sounds like she's ordering him.

"One of the sisters shares the light with a Selell. Zill shares the sun with this one."

"So they're bonded?"

Derek takes a long time to answer. "They just share the sun. That's all." Surprisingly, he sounds defiant. I've never heard him speak in that tone. "And we don't know why yet."

"I think we're bonded," Vayle says, sneering at Derek, who sneers back.

"I don't think so," Derek counters.

"I do," Vayle insists. "It makes sense. That's why we have such a *physical* connection."

"That's what you Selells do best, right? Seduce? But seducing her kind doesn't give you a connection. It makes you a creep."

A long, continuous growl is trapped in Vayle's throat. Derek steps up to him, and they stand nose to nose. I'm in an awkward position, standing right beside their showdown.

"Hey!" Deanna sounds really stern. She

commands their attention. This is definitely a side of her I've never seen. "The light connection with the Selell. You're talking about Cl'auta?"

"Clarity?" I ask.

Derek, Mr. Lux, and Deanna snap their attention to me.

"Gon me du lej'k?" Deanna says.

"Yes, I can understand." She asked if I understood her, but it was more like, *do you now hear* in English.

Deanna takes my shoulders and looks me dead in the eyes. "Zillael, you're ready."

"Ready for what?"

"Vampire," she asks, still looking into my eyes, "what do you know about the Life Blood?"

Vayle and I give each other a quick but confused glance.

"What's Life Blood?" he asks.

The next thing I know, Deanna has him by the neck and is squeezing. Even with her slender, five-feet, four-inch frame, she looks so powerful, as if her hand can crush his neck into mush.

"I'm going to ask you one more time. What do you know about the Life Blood?" she asks.

I'm bewildered. Where's my petite, blonde

mother who couldn't hurt a fly but could negotiate extra life between a snake and a ferret?

"I'm not going to remove your hand from my throat because Zillael loves you," Vayle says past clenched teeth.

"Mom, can you stop, please?" I beg her.

She looks at me, and without debate, she puts her hand down. That was too easy.

"I don't know much about being what I am," Vayle admits.

"This just happened to him last year," I add.

"Wek," Deanna calls.

"It's true," Derek confirms.

"Do you know the name of the vampire who did this to you?"

Sadness colors Vayle's expression. He says, "No," but I don't believe him.

"You know a human can't become a vampire unless they sacrifice their blood. Did you sacrifice your blood?" Deanna asks, continuing her interrogation.

"I don't know. Maybe." Vayle looks so confused.

"What happened?" I ask. My tone is tender, and when I glance at Derek, he's staring at me again.

"It was my birthday. There were these strippers,

and Dan must've slipped me something. I can't remember the rest."

Deanna nods as if she knows the scenario all too well. "You were drugged. I heard three Selells were trying to feed on you, which means you were changed by an old generation vampire."

"What does that mean?" It sounds as though nobody in the room will attempt to kill Vayle, so I walk over to the couch to sit. Vayle does the same.

Derek narrows his eyes at us. "I have to go."

Before I know it, he shoots out of the room. I chase after him, forgetting we were engaged in a discussion that would've given me more insight into Vayle and why we're so connected. Derek is moving fast, but I catch up with him in the forest that would be a twenty-minute walk away for a normal person.

"Derek!" I see him moving about fifty meters ahead of me.

He stops dead in his tracks.

"Derek." Then I'm standing right behind him. "Nothing happened between us."

"You're not telling me the truth, Zill. I can smell him on you," he says calmly.

"We kissed, but that's it."

He stands with his back to me. I think he's only seconds from running away from me again, and I swear that I'll let him go. I think I've broken his heart.

Instead, he spins around to face me. "I'm not supposed to do this."

"Do what?"

Before I know it, Derek Firth, the Wek, has his arms wrapped around me, and I think we're kissing. My eyes are closed, but my feet are off the ground. My head is floating away from my shoulders. I feel as if my mouth can't get deep enough into his. My whole body wants to merge into his.

Time passes, and we're on the ground—the snow-covered ground mixed with twigs, dead leaves, and mud. We're getting wet, and it's cold as heck, but I don't care. I don't want to stop. *I never ever want to stop.* I think Derek feels the same way.

Then a thick fog flows over us. Before I know it, Derek pulls me up, and we're both on our feet.

"Let's get back to the house," he whispers. He holds my hand as we race through the brush, breaking the record for my fastest speed ever.

"The fog means vampires, right?" I say as we break out of the tree line.

Derek stops, and I stop with him. "They're close, Zillael."

He somehow maneuvers us until we're standing

back to back. Suddenly we're joined by a third body. It's Vayle. The fog spreads over us. We can hardly see two feet ahead of us, and another body joins our circle. It's Deanna.

"We keep her safe, Wek," she whispers to Derek.

"Yes," Derek and Vayle say at the same time and then look at each other.

"I can fight, you know," I say.

"Don't do anything stupid," Deanna warns me.

I roll my eyes. I mean really, nothing's changed. I've never been a delicate little girl who needs people to fight her battles.

"Wait." Deanna tenses up.

She's right next to me, and I sense that she's listening to something far off. We're all standing as still as possible. I hear the rustling in the woods, then screams all around us. A wall of wind hits us. It's strong, but it doesn't move us a bit. After a moment, it feels as if we've been caught in the eye of the storm because all the air somehow curves around us and blows past us.

It lasts for about a minute. When the wind subsides, all the fog is gone. Even the sun is visible. Instinctively, we all look at Vayle.

"I'm not toast," he says and throws up his hands.

I sigh in relief. "What happened?"

"It's the one with the power of the force," Derek answers.

"Who's that? And what does that mean?" I ask.

"Whoa. Zill, look," Vayle says, gazing straight ahead.

I whisper, "Oh my God."

Two women are walking toward us. One is dressed in black pants, a black long-sleeved shirt, and shiny black shoes. She catches my eye because of the contrast of the black against her glowing brown skin. The other woman is just as stunning. She's wearing fitted jeans, a long white sweater, and knee-high black boots. Her hair is a ginger color and her skin rosy. They're basically upon us, and I see that their eyes are the same green as Derek's. Both women have graceful, swan-like necks. Other than skin color, they—*we*—look identical. They smile at me.

"Cl'auta and Falu," Derek whispers.

"That's Clarity and Fawn?" I ask, but they're already right in front of us.

"Yes, I'm Clarity," the one wearing black says.

"I'm Fawn," the one in the white sweater says.

"We're your sisters," Clarity says.

"But I don't understand," I say.

"How about we talk over a cup of Goshem tea?" Clarity asks.

After a long moment, I nod. I know that this is it. My time has come. My future away from Moonridge has just begun.